UNTIL WE FALL

Until We Fall

Nicole Zelniker

JADED IBIS PRESS

Published by Jaded Ibis Press.

www.jadedibispress.com

JADED IBIS PRESS

*For Michelle, who somehow
thought it would be a good idea for
me to write dystopian fiction.*

"When you're living on your knees you rise up."
—Anthony Ramos, *Hamilton*

"No you won't fool the children of the revolution."
—*T.Rex, "Children of the Revolution"*

Part I: The Run

Prologue

When Morgan limped into the living room without crutches for the first time, her parents both disengaged from the TV and shot her wide smiles, making her flinch. "There she is," her father said, standing to embrace her. He always was the more understanding of the two of them. When Morgan had expressed her desire over two years ago now to fight in the Civil War, he was the one who helped her navigate the paperwork, though reluctantly. Her mother didn't understand. She asked why Morgan cared, and screamed and cried until Morgan left for the front lines. They didn't speak much about it now.

Morgan glanced over her father's shoulder at the TV, where the president was rejoicing in his side's victory months after the fact. She felt a boiling rage toward the man, who was recently elected for a third term. *Elected* being perhaps too strong a word when a country's elections were as asinine as hers were.

She watched him spew nonsense about "family values" and felt her stomach churn. It was all a lie, to rally support. Unless the president's new definition of family values meant tearing families apart with brutalities and arrests. But her side could hardly argue against family values without looking like the bad guys.

How many new laws away were they from living in total submission to a totalitarian regime?

"I'm going back to my room," Morgan said, glancing again at the TV. If she had to watch this guy a moment longer, she was going to scream.

"Oh, honey, we can turn it off," her mother said, hitting the button on the remote. "Come sit with us."

Morgan bit her lip, but she did sit on the arm of the couch, stretching her leg out in front of her. "What was he saying?" she asked, nodding at the now black screen.

Her parents exchanged glances. "You don't need to worry about that now," her father said.

Walks were supposed to be good for her at this stage of her recovery, so she went to the park early each morning, before anyone else was there. Today, like every other day, the police were there. They were always everywhere it seemed. Her friend Herman, in fact, had been arrested in the park for loitering.

Herman had fought alongside Morgan in the war, but while Morgan returned to her parents' home, Herman didn't have anywhere to go but the park. Morgan screamed at the officer who arrested him. "What is he doing to you?" she demanded.

The officer slapped her across the face and sent her sprawling, her left knee, injured in the war, suddenly unable to support her. When Herman moved toward her to see if she was ok, the officer grabbed him and put him in handcuffs. It had been weeks since then. She didn't know how to even begin finding Herman.

Morgan exhaled, her breath just visible in the crisp air. There were already alterations to her world. The police presence and a new branch of law enforcement called Militum. A crackdown on homelessness, on poverty. Herman wasn't the only person she knew who was arrested for being homeless. Entire camps were being raided, and the people who lived there taken away. She learned this from the news. Then the media outlets she watched were shut down for criticizing the president.

Everything was falling apart. She watched two Militum officers laugh at something a third had said, as though they hadn't spent the last few weeks tearing her world apart. All three of them kept a hand on their guns, as though anticipating an attack.

Chapter One

The day Isla's favorite teacher was arrested started out fairly normal—though, Isla wouldn't actually learn of Ms. Young's arrest until months later. That day, she went to last period American history, her new favorite subject under Ms. Young, who didn't shy away from the truth. Before senior year, Isla hadn't known anything about the Second Civil War beyond that there was one. It was the line all her previous teachers parroted, anyway. There was a civil war and we won it, thanks to President Powers, then just a military commander.

Some time ago, Isla and her younger sister, Hannah, asked their parents about the war. She must have been thirteen or fourteen, Hannah eleven or twelve. Their mom had made dinner, probably spaghetti or mac and cheese. She always made something vegetarian, since Isla didn't eat meat and it was hard enough making one meal. Their dad used to make dinner, before it became harder for women to find work and he had to take on longer hours at the lab. Now, it was the running joke that the worst chef in the family made all the meals.

"But why can't Mom go back to work?" Isla asked. Hannah frowned.

"It's complicated," their mother said. When Isla and Hannah were really young, she was a lawyer. After the war, the president thought it made more sense to have a parent at home. Now, she advised legal firms, but only while the girls were in school. She was good at it, true, but it wasn't her passion. It wasn't standing up in the courtroom and demanding justice. As much as she tried to hide it, her girls knew she wasn't happy.

"Why was there a war anyway?" Hannah asked.

"You aren't learning about it in school?" their dad asked, pushing overcooked vegetables around on his plate.

Hannah shook her head, and their parents exchanged glances. Their father said, "I guess it was mostly about family values, right?" That was the first time Isla realized that maybe her parents didn't have all the answers.

Senior year, though, Ms. Young taught Isla about how the president before Powers declared himself ruler during the Civil War, how he passed the mantle down after abolishing elections. At that point, he had already replaced nine of the twelve members of the Supreme Court with his own men. Now, all of the judges were Powers' plants.

Then Ms. Young looked around at her students' blank faces—there were nine others in Isla's AP History class—and realized she had to explain what the Supreme Court was.

"It's like, you know how when you're charged with doing something wrong, you go to court before a judge, and they decide your punishment? The Supreme Court is kind of like that, but only when the wrong thing has to do with the constitution. So if a boss fires someone for being gay, let's say, the employee can take the case all the way up to the Supreme Court under the —"

"But Ms. Young," one of the students interrupted. Danny Bose, a boy with a narrow stare, whom Isla particularly loathed, had his hand in the air and his mouth open, like he was going to speak whether Ms. Young called on him or not.

Ms. Young's nostrils flared, and her eyes narrowed slightly. "Yes, Danny."

"Being gay is illegal though," he said with a slight glance at Isla, who flushed. She wasn't even gay, but she had a strange feeling Danny knew she was trans, like he could smell she didn't belong. Both were illegal. She only knew what it meant to be trans because of her parents. And she knew she was lucky she could "pass" without surgery, whatever that really meant.

Ms. Young twisted her dark hair up in a bun and let it fall again. Without looking at her students, she said, "Just because something is illegal doesn't mean it's wrong."

Isla stayed after class often, since it was the last period of the day. She liked Ms. Young. She liked the way she thought about things and the way she explained them to the class. And Isla suspected that even if she did come out to Ms. Young, Ms. Young wouldn't report her.

"Honestly, they teach you less and less every year," Ms. Young said. "I've never had to explain the Supreme Court to AP students before."

"We know most of it," Isla said, her cheeks hot. It was a lie, but she didn't want to seem stupid in front of Ms. Young. She had the feeling Ms. Young wasn't supposed to be teaching them about most of this anyway. The idea sent a small thrill through her—she knew something the other students didn't.

"I don't mean any offense by it," Ms. Young said. "It's the curriculum. They don't want you to know anything."

"But why?" They were sitting behind Ms. Young's desk. It was sparse, the desk, with only a laptop and spiral notebook resting on the pale wood. There was no picture of a husband or family, even though Ms. Young wore a wedding ring. Isla had stayed on the premise of asking Ms. Young a question about the homework, but really, she just felt safe in the classroom, like she was welcome there.

She loved the old maps showing what the U.S. looked like before California split from the nation not long before the end of the Civil War. The maps with fifty states instead of fifteen. Ms. Young told her that California was only allowed to split because it meant a complete takeover would be easier. The states were redrawn to facilitate stronger conservative voting blocks. Isla still wasn't entirely sure why that mattered.

On the old maps, Evanston was marked in red and Wisconsiowa, formerly multiple states, was highlighted around the border. She loved the books in the back of the class, even though Ms. Young assured her there was nothing there she would want to read. She loved having someone she could ask questions of who would actually give her an answer worth hearing.

"It's . . . well, I was going to say it's complicated, but I guess it isn't. They don't want you to know because it's messed up. The way—"

Someone knocked on the door then and cracked it open. "Ms. Young? May I speak with you?"

"Of course," Ms. Young said, standing. Principal Tanner opened the door and strode into the room and nodded briefly at Isla. To Ms. Young, he said, "In my office, please?"

"Sure." She offered Isla a small smile and left the room, leaving Isla alone.

Later that night, Isla shared what she'd learned with her

sister. They sat in Hannah's bedroom, where stars decorated the ceiling and astronomy posters the walls. Of the two of them, Hannah had picked up their father's passion for the stars. Truly, Hannah was a genius when it came to astronomy, and really anything else that had to do with science or math. Her teachers were already encouraging her to apply for colleges, and she'd won several academic awards in the last year alone. Though two years younger than Isla, she was only one year below in school because she skipped second grade. She had been taking her math and science courses at the local university for the last year.

Their parents had gone to bed after watching Powers on TV extolling the virtues of some new policy Isla couldn't remember the name of but knew it had to do with giving the Militum more power. Earlier that week, Isla and Hannah's neighbors had been arrested by a group of Militum officers. Isla heard they were part of the rebellion, that another neighbor found them out. Isla was astounded to think of Mr. and Mrs. Majd as rebels. In her mind, they were the nice older couple who baked cookies sometimes and who had let Isla and Hannah play in their yard when the girls were younger. But she supposed she never really knew them well at all.

The two girls sat crisscross on the bed, facing each other. "It wasn't always illegal," Isla told Hannah, repeating what Ms. Young told her after class. "Apparently, it was actually illegal to fire people for being gay."

"Damn," Hannah said. She twisted a handful of braids in her hand, tapping the ends together and making the beads that rested there clack.

"Do you think—I mean, never mind. I forgot what I was going to say."

"No, you didn't." Hannah slid closer to Isla on the bed.

"What?"

"It's not important."

Hannah pursed her lips. "Isla Logan, you tell me right now."

"Oh, you look so much like Mom."

"C'mon—"

"I was just . . . just wondering if you thought they might be able to tell at school . . . ."

Hannah waited for Isla to say more, but she didn't. Hannah frowned. "That you're trans?" Isla nodded, and Hannah didn't say anything else, just snuggled in close to Isla and held her tight.

Ms. Young wasn't in class the next day. Or the rest of the week. The formerly barren trees grew thick with pink flowers and green leaves, and Ms. Young never came back to class. There were substitute teachers at first, all of whom seemed to have a special disdain for Isla herself. Then one of the subs, a woman called Ms. Greene, told them that she was a permanent replacement.

Isla stopped by Principal Tanner's office after school that day and found his secretary still there, finishing a crossword puzzle on her phone. Isla knew Mrs. Ruiz well, since several boys had tried to beat Isla up on the playground or called her slurs, some about being gay, some about being Black, in class over the four years she was a student there. She was always brought to the office with the boys, even when she hadn't done anything wrong. Most of the time, she didn't even fight back. Whenever she was there, Mrs. Ruiz slipped her sweets or gave her a wink. "How are you today, Ms. Logan?" Mrs. Ruiz asked, looking up from her phone.

"I'm okay," Isla said, offering her a small smile in return. "I was just wondering if I could ask Principal Tanner a question."

Mrs. Ruiz hesitated. "Is it . . . it's about Ms. Young, isn't it?"

"Yes," Isla said. There was no point in pretending.

"She's not coming back. She quit last month."

Isla's heart fell into her stomach. "She just quit? Just like that?"

"I'm sorry, dear," Mrs. Ruiz said. "She was a great teacher."

"I . . . thank you." Isla gripped the straps on her backpack and left the office. She didn't cry until she reached the bathroom. She locked herself in a stall and sobbed.

Chapter Two

Morgan Young knew that joining the revolution was a risk. She also knew she had to take it. Much of what they did took place underground, literally—often in members' basements or secret hideaways. (Her friend Adam hosted meetings in an abandoned warehouse, with concrete slabs instead of couches. Once at a winter meeting, she had sustained burns on her hands from the ice that covered the concrete.) And now, several of the people she consorted with were being watched by the government.

Shane, Morgan's husband, didn't have as much to do with the revolution, but he supported her being a part of it, to an extent. She knew they'd probably hurt her Black husband far worse than they would hurt her, a white woman, if she were caught. Honestly, part of her was secretly glad that Shane didn't involve himself like she did. She didn't transport people to the border anymore, since she had a full-time job, but she transported a lot of messages back and forth and identified recruits.

Her favorite part of the work, though, was the teaching, even if it wasn't technically part of it and even if she only initially took the job because it was one of the few that women could still do. She loved the look on a student's face when they realized there was more than what they'd been told. In earlier years, she'd gotten several of them to do work for her co-conspirators—after they graduated, of course. Now, not so much.

"We know most of it," Isla Logan protested, sitting with Morgan after class, when Morgan told her she'd never before had to explain the Supreme Court to AP students. Isla often stayed after class, but Morgan didn't mind. It had been a long time since she had a student who actually wanted to learn.

A knock on the door, and then Joey Tanner opened it. "Ms. Young? May I speak with you?"

"Of course." Mr. Tanner glanced at Isla and clarified, "In my office, please?"

Shit.

"Sure," she said, and she left, giving Isla a small smile on her way out.

In his office, Tanner said, "I wanted to give you the chance to explain yourself."

"Explain?"

"I know you're part of the rebellion," he said, sitting behind his desk now. "The resistance. Whatever. Someone saw you going to a known rebel's house and called me."

Morgan kept her face blank. She always knew this would happen eventually. Her husband had pleaded with her repeatedly to stop her work for this exact reason. So many of the people she knew had lost their jobs. Some of them were arrested. Others fled. "I don't understand."

"Please, just tell me why."

She had a choice now. She could beg forgiveness, tell Tanner she was coerced, and continue to teach. She'd made so much progress with several of her students already. She thought of Isla, who had so many questions and who was so excited to learn. How could she leave now?

On the other hand, there was little to no chance Tanner would believe her. And what kind of person would she be if she didn't speak her mind, if she didn't tell this man who clearly didn't care that his complacency was only hurting people? She would have to leave, but she could start over. And what sort of example was she setting for her students if she didn't speak her mind?

If only she knew what the right choice was. Finally, she said, "Because everything is fucked."

Mr. Tanner sighed through his nose. "I see." He met her eyes. "I'm sorry." That was the day Morgan lost her job.

"I don't presume you'll stop," Shane said. "With the revolution."

Morgan toyed with the spaghetti on her plate, pushing it around with her fork. "Of course not."

"It's dangerous." Already, they were discussing relocating. It wouldn't be the first time someone from the revolution was forced to flee from their home in the dead of night.

"I know. That's why I have to do it." She put her fork down and looked her husband in the eyes. "It's so dangerous because they don't want us revolting. The president is scared of us."

Morgan flinched at a knock on their door. *Not again.* Shane squeezed her hand and got up to answer it. On the other side, two Militum officers stood in uniform. They never wore their names or their badge numbers on their outfits, but all the officers wore pale blue. "Shane Wilson and Morgan Young?" It was an ongoing point of contention with many of Morgan's colleagues and so-called friends that she didn't take

Shane's last name, but he didn't mind.

Shane took a step back. "Yes?"

The officers stepped inside. "You're both under arrest for conspiring to take down the regime."

Morgan looked over at Shane, horrified. "No!"

"Your boss—"

"No, I mean Shane has nothing to do with it," she said. "He never—"

"Ma'am," the other officer stepped toward her, handcuffs ready, "if your husband never reported you, he's guilty of—"

"He didn't know," Morgan lied. "He never suspected anything."

"We'll sort this all out at the courthouse," the first officer said. He now had Shane in cuffs.

"It's ok," he said, but she could read the fear in his eyes. His hands rattled against the cuffs.

"Look, Christian—"

"Officer Shore."

"Right." This guy was how old, maybe twenty? At most twenty-one? She was already a veteran when this kid was born. "Officer Shore, I already told you. I'm not giving away the names of anyone I've worked with."

"Really, Ms. Young, we're trying to cooperate with you here," Shore said. "I—"

"I want a lawyer."

Shore started laughing, cackling almost. The sound forced Morgan's heart into her mouth. "You won't get a lawyer. Are you kidding?"

"It's the law, Officer," she said, sitting back in the interrogation chair, crossing one leg over her lap and feigning calm. Someone had loosened one of the legs so that the chair tipped precariously to the side, and Morgan had to work to keep her balance.

"Not for rebels," he told her, smirking slightly. "You've already confessed. Unless you give us those names, you're about to rot in jail, sweetheart."

Morgan's foot fell back to the floor. She glared up at Officer Shore. "Fuck you."

"Welp," Shore said, signaling to someone behind the glass. "So be it." A second officer entered and put Morgan back in handcuffs, tightening them so that they cut into her wrists. She glared at both of them, but did nothing else. She wouldn't show them her fear, even if she felt it in overwhelming waves.

* * *

Isla hated coming to school now. Ms. Greene ranted daily about how good and strong and right President Powers was, and Danny Bose and his friends teased her worse than ever. She kept her head down and stayed quiet in her classes. After, she often walked home alone, since Hannah was in so many clubs. She liked to go through the park, especially as the weather got nicer, though her parents were always worried about her getting too close to the next town over, the "bad neighborhood."

It wasn't like she could talk about much to her parents anyway. Not that they would ever rat her out to the government or anything. It was Isla's parents who had insisted the family move to Evanston, so Isla could start over as the woman she was, who allowed her to be herself to the extent that they could. In the interim, they homeschooled her themselves. But she didn't want them to know more than they had to. She didn't want to get them in trouble should something happen to her, whatever that something might be.

She was thinking about this as a movie played in her history class, one they had all seen about their country's recent history. She glanced up occasionally and listened to Powers railing against the gays that were "ruining their country" and "spreading their sinful ways." It made her want to vomit. She took a deep breath instead and tried to recall all Ms. Young had taught them about separation of church and state. Then she remembered Ms. Young had left her.

"God made men and women to be together," Powers was saying. "And to deny that truth is un-Ameri—" The lights came up as two Militum officers came into the class, causing the students around Isla to start whispering frantically. It was almost a welcome distraction.

Then they called her name.

All of her classmates stared at her, at her wide eyes and dropped jaw. Hesitantly, she stood. "That's me."

"Come with us, please." The officers moved to the side so that she could leave the classroom. She glanced up at Ms. Greene, who made no motion to stop her. She didn't have a choice. Isla followed the officers.

Out of the corner of her eye, she saw another classroom door open and someone run toward her down the hallway. "Isla?"

She turned around, fear forcing her stomach to clench. "Hannah?"

The officers on either side of her moved to stand between Isla and her sister. Hannah stopped suddenly, her eyebrows contracted in confusion.

"Hannah, it's ok," Isla said, even though she had no idea what was going on. "Go back to class."

She didn't. "Where are you taking my sister?"

"That's none of your concern," one of the officers said. "Go back to class." The officers walked forward, urging Isla on. She looked back before she turned the corner. Hannah was still there, poised to run after her.

Down at the precinct, the officer that questioned Isla was young, maybe a few years older than she was. Was it weird that she was excited to see a Black Militum officer? They almost always looked nothing like her, and honestly, she felt safer with someone who might understand just a little bit of what her own life was like. But maybe that was just silly.

At first, she was afraid someone had outed her. But she quickly realized the officers had no idea that she was trans, that when she presented her ID, her parents' false documents held up.

So that meant they were really asking about the revolution. But why her? She didn't know anything.

He introduced himself as Officer Shore. "We need to ask you a few questions about a woman named Morgan Young."

Isla's heart pounded. "I thought she quit," Isla said.

"Did you?" Officer Shore asked. He was standing with his hands on the back of his chair. "Interesting."

Isla frowned. "What is?"

"We hear from our sources that you and Ms. Young were very close."

A small lump formed in Isla's throat. "I thought so," she said.

"And you really had no idea that she and her husband were agents for the rebellion?"

Isla blinked. "What? No. I had no idea." How could she have known? How could she have not?

"Look, this will be a lot easier for you if you tell us the truth."

"I am!" Isla nearly jumped to her feet before she realized that might not be a good idea.

"Hmm. Then how come a neighbor saw you going into the home of a known rebel?" Shore slapped a photo on the table between them. Someone around Isla's height and weight was in the photo, true, but—

"That's not me," Isla said. "Those aren't my clothes, and I've never permed my hair like that." Who could have accused her?

Shore sighed, and Isla frowned. Why wouldn't he listen? "I'm truly disappointed in you," Shore said. "I really thought you would cooperate with us."

"I'm trying to," Isla protested. "But I don't—"

"Never mind," Shore said, waving to the mirror behind them. "I'm sure you'll talk eventually." Another officer came into the room with handcuffs then, and Isla realized what was about to happen.

"Wait, no!"

The Militum officer took her hands and cuffed her, each side making a soft click as it closed around her wrist, pinching her skin. Isla's lip trembled. "You can't do this."

Shore's shoulders tensed. "I can," he said. "And I will." The second officer pushed Isla forward, and she stumbled, but she never looked away from Christian Shore. His green eyes followed her until she rounded the corner on her way to the cells.

Chapter Three

Hannah's parents were sick with worry. They spent days on the phone with local police, who could tell them nothing. At night she heard them crying in their room. All they knew of Isla's whereabouts was what Hannah had told them, which wasn't much.

The Saturday after Isla was taken, Hannah went down to the police station, but they turned her away. She kept going back. The next day. After school on Monday. And on Tuesday. On Wednesday, she met a sympathetic officer, Dex Sherman, named after the president, and he told her that Isla wasn't there.

"Where is she?"

Dex's eyes wandered to the side of Hannah's face, his desk, anywhere that wasn't her eyes. "There's a prison in Evanston for traitors to the state."

"Excuse me, what?"

"The prisoner—"

"Isla."

"Is accused of aiding and abetting terrorists."

Hannah blinked. Isla, abetting terrorism? The thought was at best laughable. She glared at Sherman until he finally met her eyes. "Where in Evanston?" she asked.

Every fresh breeze, every bird call, every rustle of the leaves— it all set Hannah on edge. She didn't even know if she was allowed to be there, at the prison her sister resided in. But she figured it was better to ask forgiveness than permission, at least in this case.

The prison itself was surrounded by guards and around the guards, barbed wire. The windows were all barred, and they were hardly windows besides: They were narrow and slanted, letting in just enough oxygen to prevent the people inside from suffocating on stale air.

What had Isla done? Hannah couldn't figure that out. If Isla had joined a group of rebels, Hannah surely would have known. But if she didn't, how did she end up at this high-security government prison? Did the officer lie to her?

A twig snapped. Hannah whirled around, but it was only a squirrel, already dashing away. She glared at it. "You're not Militum," she grumbled.

"No, but I am."

Hannah startled. Before her stood a man in a navy uniform, his pale face cloaked in a neatly trimmed, raven-black beard. She hadn't heard him approach. "S-sorry, I was lost and—"

"Dex called," the man interrupted. "He told me you were coming. Hannah, right?"

Her blood ran cold. "Are you going to arrest me?"

The man shook his head. "Come with me," he said.

Hannah didn't move. "Do I have a choice?" she asked.

The man shrugged. "You always have a choice," he said. "Just not if you want to free your sister."

The man's name was Farlen, and he was a Militum lieutenant. He was also an agent for the revolution.

Hannah set her glass down. Farlen had taken her to a rec center about a fifteen-minute drive from the prison, where he said local agents met in the basement. Since no one was there, they sat at the island in the kitchen with another woman, who had served her water and offered her a peach. The peach sat untouched.

"You're a spy," Hannah said.

The woman laughed. "I guess you are," she said to Farlen. "That makes you sound a lot cooler than you are."

Farlen grinned. "Ignore Temi," he told Hannah. "She's harmless."

"Why are you telling me all of this?" Hannah asked.

"It's a risk," Farlen agreed. "But you want your sister out. We have some others in that prison we'd like to free. I think we can help each other."

Hannah looked back and forth between these two strangers, Farlen and Temi, asking her to commit a crime against the government. She had no reason to trust them. But they weren't the ones who arrested Isla, and they were willing to help Hannah set her free.

Like Farlen said, she always had a choice. So she made one.

"Ok," Hannah said. "What do you need?"

Temi leaned forward on her elbows. "We looked you up," Temi said. "You've won all kinds of awards. Science, building things."

Hannah forced herself to meet Temi's eyes. "Ok?"

"Have you ever built a bomb, Hannah?"

* * *

Isla had run out of tears. The first few days, it seemed all she could do was cry. Now, she was hollow. She lived in fear that the Militum would move her before her family could find her, or that she would never see her family again, or that they would figure out that she was trans and she would suffer worse punishment. Still, she couldn't bring herself to cry.

Footsteps echoed down the hall. Usually the guards left her well enough alone, but this one stopped outside her door. "Isla Logan, come with me."

Isla stood. She held her hands out so the lieutenant could put cuffs on her. Then he opened the door to her cell, and she followed him down to the basement.

The lieutenant locked the door behind him. Isla's heart leapt into her throat. The light in the basement was dim, nearly dark. She was surrounded by boxes, piled high. She wanted to ask why they were down there, but she knew better.

At last, the lieutenant leaned in close to her. "I'm working with your sister," he whispered. "We're going to get you out of here."

A beat. Isla stared at this man she didn't know. She had never seen him in the prison before. "I'm sorry?"

"Speak more softly, if you don't mind. The walls have ears here." He looked over his shoulder, then back at Isla. "I'm an agent for the revolution. A few weeks ago, we began a plan to release all the people in this prison. We finally found someone who can help us with the last piece."

"Hannah," she realized. The thought left her breathless. What was Hannah doing working with a group of rebels? How did she even find her?

"Tomorrow, the prison is going to explode. We're going

to blow the side of the cells wide open. Your sister will be in the woods behind the prison, waiting for you with bikes. I promised her I'd pass along the message."

"Wait, you're going to blow up the prison?"

"The walls. No one here will get hurt. We have too many valuable people inside now, and we need to get them out."

"How did you even find my sister?" Isla whispered. "How did she find me? What did you tell her?"

"She can answer all of those questions for you when you see her again. We've been down here too long already."

The lieutenant turned away from her, but Isla grabbed his sleeve. "Wait," she said. "Would it be possible to get a message to someone else? Another prisoner?"

He nodded. "Who?"

"Morgan Young," Isla said. "She can come with us."

"Morgan Young is in solitary," he said. "But I could get a message to her husband."

*   *   *

For Morgan, the most difficult place to be was inside her own head. It was the only place her tiny solitary cell allowed her to go. The place Morgan spent her days and nights was just wide enough that she could spread her arms out and touch both walls with her fingertips and long enough for a bed meant for someone several inches shorter than her. The walls were stone: The steel door housed the only window through which she would sometimes peer out into the hallway, not entirely sure what she was waiting for.

It gave her time to think about Shane. About how the same man who had stayed by her side through her post-war recovery, who held her when she woke screaming from disjointed nightmares, who baked bread on his days off and cried at sappy movies, now rotted in a cell of his own. She asked every guard that passed by how and where Shane was. She never got an answer.

Solitary forced her back into the field, where she watched her comrades drop dead on a loop, or worse, linger. It brought her back to the moment she'd been shot and after, when she lay in agony for days before they sent her home to lie in agony elsewhere. It brought her back to the tent several days before her injury, surrounded by twelve men from her own unit—

No. She couldn't think about that.

Morgan did think about her students, though, and what they must have been told. They either thought she was a terrorist, a traitor to their country, or else they were told nothing. She wasn't sure which was worse.

In fact, Morgan was thinking about her students when her world exploded.

* * *

Hannah shielded her eyes as the bombs went off, each seconds after the one before it. Another moment and a shadow appeared from the smoke.

"Isla!" She could barely hear her own voice over the roaring of the flames and the sirens now blaring. Isla reached her seconds later and wrapped Hannah in the strongest hug she could. "Are you alright?"

Hannah pulled away. "Ms. Young . . ."

From the smoke, two outlines emerged: A man Hannah didn't know hand in hand with Morgan Young. Both of them were coughing hard. The man—Shane was his name, or so Farlen said—spat something black onto the ground and cried,

"Go!"

The girls sprinted away from the prison and hopped on their bikes, Hannah leading. Farlen and Temi had helped her bring two others over, and Morgan and Shane grabbed them, close behind the girls. Hannah knew Shane could easily overtake them, but he didn't know how to get where they were going. A good twenty minutes later, they were all gasping for air on the Logan's stoop. Morgan steadied herself against the railing and said, "Can anyone tell me what the hell is going on?"

"No time," Hannah wheezed. "You've gotta get to the cellar. I'll move the bikes after."

Isla motioned for Morgan and Shane to follow them around back, behind the house, where Isla removed a thin panel of wood that nearly blended into the wall. Hannah went in first, followed by Shane, who was nearly too big. Morgan followed, letting her eyes adjust to the dark as Isla descended behind her. The wall across from the almost-window was lined with canned goods: soups and beans and vegetables. In the middle of the room stood a short table supporting a shorter stack of books and a lamp that Isla was lighting with a book of matches. Next to the hole they had used to get into the bunker was a rifle.

"What is this place?" Shane asked.

"It was like this when we moved in," Hannah said. "Our parents don't talk about it much, but I heard my mom say someone must've hidden refugees here once." Hannah's eyes fell on the table. "Oh, and the books and the lamp I added. I didn't want you to get bored. We'll have to move you as soon as possible, but I think we should wait a few days. The Militum might come here since Isla broke out, but they don't know about this place."

Hannah watched Morgan scan the titles. Most of them, including My Life: A Memoir by Dexter Powers, had come from her father's study, the only place she could get books. "Thank you," Morgan said, turning away from Powers' photo on the top of the pile.

"Thank Isla," Hannah said. "She's the one who wanted to get you guys out." To Isla, she said, "I'll come back as soon as I can, ok?" Isla nodded, but Hannah stayed a moment longer.

What if something happened and she couldn't get back?

*　*　*

Isla watched Ms. Young survey the room again—food, books, gun—as she spoke. Isla explained how Hannah had built a bomb to free them. She still didn't know the lieutenant's name, but she told them how she'd asked him to get in touch with Morgan. Shane confirmed that the man found him. That was how he found Hannah and Isla.

At last, Isla finished and asked one of her own questions. "Are you really part of the rebellion?"

"Revolution," Morgan corrected. "Shane isn't, but I am."

"Why?"

"Why? Because no one should tell us how to live just because of who we love," Morgan said. She turned away from Isla, but Isla still heard the tremble in her voice. "Because no one should have their rights to their own body taken away from them. Because the way most people are treated in this country is messed up."

Isla contemplated this for a moment, silent. No one had ever explained it to her like that before. Then she asked, "Did you fight in the Civil War?" Her own parents hadn't, though they were old enough.

"Yes." Morgan gestured between her and Shane. "Both of us."

"She's flattering me," Shane said to Isla. "I was a medic."

"You saved me."

"You wouldn't have died," Shane said, but he looked uncomfortable when he said it.

"You saved my leg, at least." To Isla, she said, "I am sorry. I never meant to get you involved in this mess."

"It's ok," Isla said. "I'm ok now." Another pause and then she said, "So the Civil War wasn't really about family values?" She couldn't imagine why someone would fight against that.

"No. That's a line they parrot to make people think they care. The Civil War was about a small group of men seizing power and keeping the rest of us down." Morgan stood up suddenly. "What was that?"

"What?" But then Isla heard it, too. A gun shot. And then another one.

Chapter Four

Hannah had just fallen asleep when a sharp BANG! BANG! BANG! at the front door jolted her awake. Then her parents' footsteps and low voices. "Who could that be?"

She crept after them as quietly as she could, avoiding the creakiest floorboards on instinct. She hovered at the top of the stairs and listened to her parents let someone into the house. More than one someone, based on the footsteps. She tried to quiet her breath, but it seemed so loud in her own ears. "Mr. and Mrs. Logan?" *Militum.*

"Yes?" That was Hannah's father. Hannah grabbed at her arms in a false hug, her nails digging into her skin.

"We have some questions for you," another man said. "If you wouldn't mind—"

"Our daughter is asleep upstairs," Hannah's mother said. "We can't just—"

"Mrs. Logan, with all due respect, we're not asking." Hannah heard the door shut.

"Is this about Isla?" Mr. Logan asked. "Where is she? Where's Isla?"

"Mr. Logan, please."

Hannah felt a painful twisting in her gut at those words and crept quietly down another stair. "Just tell us if she's ok, please." That was her mother.

"Is there anyone in the house, ma'am?"

"No. No, just us and Hannah."

The first shot echoed in Hannah's ears like thunder, reverberating so that she almost didn't hear the second. Then footsteps again, and Hannah stumbled backwards up the stairs, locking herself for a moment in the bathroom. *Breathe in, breathe out, breathe—they killed my parents.*

Hannah swallowed her rising nausea and listened, rubbing the bottom of her T-shirt between two fingers—something her mother did when she was anxious. The Militum came up the stairs; they spoke to each other in low whispers. They thought she was still asleep. She waited until she couldn't hear them anymore before silently cracking the door open.

And then she ran for it.

* * *

Morgan grabbed the rifle off the wall and immediately checked to make sure it was loaded. It was. "Stay here."

"But—"

Shane gripped Isla by the shoulder. "It's going to be ok." He glanced at Morgan, who removed the panel from the wall.

Morgan slithered out on her belly, the gun slung around her back. As soon as she could, she got back on her feet and pointed the gun in front of her. She turned the corner sharply, her eye on the scope of the gun. Morgan heard Hannah scream just before she came around the bend, pursued by two men in officers' uniforms.

"Down!" Hannah dropped to the ground, and Morgan squeezed the trigger twice. The first bullet went straight through the first officer's eye and the second through the second officer's chest. Morgan went to Hannah and dropped to her knees. "Are you ok?"

"They killed my parents." Hannah was sobbing and shaking on the ground. Morgan wasn't sure if she would be able to get up.

"Ok. Ok." Morgan ran a hand through her hair and searched her mind desperately for a solution. The officers' colleagues knew where they were, they would come after them when they failed to return to their precinct. "We have to go." She put the gun on the ground and placed her hand on Hannah's back. "We have to go, ok?"

Hannah pushed herself up, still shaking, and Morgan held her tight, letting the girl cry onto her shoulder. Behind them, the officer with a bullet in the chest twitched once, twice, and was still.

Morgan and the others pressed on as the morning dawned, nearly silent from their exhaustion. She kept a heavy-lidded eye on the younger girl, thinking she would wear down the quickest, but Hannah Logan held her own, seeming only to slow down for everyone else's sake. Her eyes were empty and far away, a look all too familiar to Morgan. That was what war did to people.

Morgan was no stranger to loss, but she had signed up for that kind of life. Hannah was about the age Morgan was when she went off to war. And Morgan had never lost a parent that way. Suddenly and violently. She lost her parents in a different way.

As noon approached and the temperature steadily rose, Morgan began to lean heavily on her right side, her left knee pulsing under her prison uniform. "We should stop," she said. "Take a rest." The others followed her into the shade, where Morgan lowered herself onto a mossy log. She stretched her left leg out in front of her and exhaled.

"Is your knee ok?" Shane murmured as he sat beside her.

"Fine." Morgan watched as the girls sat across from them, both hunched over and hollow. She glanced around at their surroundings in search of a distraction. Her eyes fell on a bush, and she felt her lips twitch into a small smile. "Have you guys ever had juneberries before?" The girls shook their heads, and Morgan picked a few off a branch. "They're sweet," she said, holding them out.

Shane and Isla both popped theirs in their mouths. Hannah took them, but only squished them in her hands, looking at them but not quite seeing. "It's not poisonous," Morgan told her. "I used to eat them all the time." To prove her point, she dropped a few berries on her tongue.

Hannah seemed to come back to earth. She blushed and hastily ate her own berries. Beside her, Isla swallowed. "Used to?"

"As a kid, I mean. My grandparents had them all over their backyard." She also used to eat them on trips transferring refugees. But the girls would learn about that soon enough.

* * *

Adam Boeck and Morgan went back just over twenty years. When Morgan attended her first meeting, she was twenty-one. Adam, just nineteen, had been attending these meetings for three years already, since the war ended. She learned that his parents came with their son to the United States from Brazil in search of better, and that when they couldn't find it here, they decided to make themselves a better place instead, going so far as to recruit their own son into the revolution when it came about.

He helped her understand what they were doing in Evanston: bringing people from the U.S. to California to escape. "But what about the people who are still here?" she asked.

"We're doing all we can," he told her. All we can included getting in touch with the UN. It included protesting and making themselves matter, even when protesting became illegal without a permit. It included educating people on their history and recruiting volunteers. In part, Morgan became a teacher when Powers prohibited women from working jobs that took them away from caring for the families, even if they didn't have children at home, to do all she could. So when Morgan found herself in trouble, Adam's place was the first one she thought of as safe.

Adam clearly wasn't expecting company. Morgan caught him peering around the curtain when she arrived with the others, presumably fearing that the Militum had found him. When he realized it was her, he ran to the door. "Morgan?"

Morgan could imagine the odd scene from Adam's perspective. There she was, standing on his doorstep with three people he'd never met. She, Shane, and Isla wore tan prison suits and torn slippers. Hannah wore an Evanston University T-shirt and faded sneakers. They all carried backpacks crammed with a change of clothes and a handful of food. "I'm sorry. It's late—"

"Are you ok? No one has heard from you in months."

"Actually, that's why I'm here." She took a breath. "They found me. They arrested me and my husband"—her hand drifted into Shane's—"and one of my students." Her other hand fell on Isla's shoulder.

"You need to get out," he said.

"That's why I came to you," Morgan said, the ghost of a smile playing on her lips. "Who better?"

"Of course I'll help," Adam said. "Come in."

* * *

Adam set them all up in his spare rooms. Isla and Hannah shared with Jiao Ming See, another refugee staying with Adam. He showed Morgan and Shane a separate room down the hall. "The bed is pretty small," Adam said. "But everything is clean, and you can shower and everything."

"It's perfect," Morgan said, giving his shoulder a squeeze. "Thank you."

While they waited for dinner, Morgan climbed into the twin bed with Shane and put her head on his chest. Her hair, still damp from her first shower in over week, cooled his bare skin. She wore a sweater and jeans that she had taken from Isla and Hannah's house, along with clothes for the rest of them. She had refused to let Hannah or Isla back into the house. Shane knew it was because their parents' bodies were somewhere visible, likely in a place Hannah had already passed on her way out.

Shane wrapped his arms around Morgan. She was smaller after these many months locked away. Thinner. He supposed he must be, too. But he had at least been able to use the exercise yard every once in a while.

She took his left hand in both of hers and traced his wedding band with a finger. "I'm sorry," she said.

He sat up a little straighter. "Why are you sorry?"

"You had nothing to do with this. You and the girls. I just—"

"Hey." He put his hand under her chin, and she looked up at him. "Stop. I wouldn't want to be anywhere else." He held her closer and breathed in her hair, which smelled vaguely of strawberries. Shane wanted to tell her that everything would be ok, that they would be ok, but he couldn't lie to Morgan. The truth was that fear had settled in the forefront of his mind and sunk in its sharp claws. It was lodged there, and no amount of reassurance would shake it free.

It was also true that if Morgan was here, this was the place for him. He couldn't imagine being without her.

Chapter Five

Jackson Shore was plenty used to press conferences at this point. All he had to do, for the most part, was stand there as a representative of the Militum and watch President Dexter Powers tell the American public that he was winning the war against the terrorists, praise God, blah, blah, blah. This time in particular, Powers would speak about the new Police Powers Act, which would give Militum officers the power to kill rebels without recourse. Of course, he would phrase it in a much nicer, more palatable way. It was for the benefit of their country, he would say. It would stop the rebels from doing any more damage. Shore thought Powers might even believe some of it.

At least a part of him believed what he said about the rebels. Once the rebels had drawn national attention, Powers' team began framing the group as violent, indiscriminate in who they hurt in their quest to seize power. They were supposed to be the anti-Militum, and what would the poor, helpless public do without the Militum?

For a while, the rebels weren't an issue. They were small, and who cared what a small opposition group did as long as they didn't make any waves? But somehow, they managed to get word of supposed human rights abuses to the UN, who were now threatening to cease trade if they weren't granted access to the said terrorists to ask about their conditions. It was all out of order, or so Powers said.

Jackson himself understood the necessity of the deception, although he didn't truly believe it. As far as family values went, there was only one family he could afford to care about: his own. And his own was doing rather well in this particular era.

Powers adjusted his microphone as he spewed nonsense about how great it was that a select group of people had such power over the masses. There were a few journalists in attendance, largely at the same newspapers Powers and his allies owned. The handful of others worked with the understanding that if they spoke out, they would be suspended, or worse, killed. One of the journalists raised a hand and asked, "President Powers, are there any security concerns regarding rebel activity?"

The big thing now was getting the people to understand that the rebels were wrong, to make people think the rebels were dangerous, and for those that didn't believe that line, that they were not worth supporting regardless. So Powers lied. "Not much," he said. "Many of them have realized their mistakes and have atoned for their crimes. The others are floundering without support."

Jackson Shore couldn't stop his eye from twitching at his words. They had to get those Evanston rebels back.

Jackson glanced around the table. At the various secretaries, of defense and war, and also in the traditional sense. In fact, he sat across from Powers' own secretary and personal assistant, Ilana Cruz. Beside him sat Trevor Sullivan, Powers' vice president as of some years ago.

The whole room stood as Powers entered, taking his seat

at the head of the table. As he sat, the others silently resumed their positions. Jackson was the slowest to do so.

"First agenda item," Powers said, "apparently the rebels are somehow sneaking anti-government books into the country and mass-producing them. Sullivan, you'll find out where they're coming from." Turning to his left, to Ilana Cruz and his press director Colin Jaspers, he said, "Ilana and Jaspers, you'll work with the press to spin the story in our favor."

"Of course, Sir," Jaspers said while Cruz typed the notes. She gave a curt nod, and Powers continued, "Now, on to other matters." Jackson cringed as Powers delivered the news: "There's been a breakout at our prison in Evanston."

* * *

Hannah and Isla were both happy to share a room with Jiao Ming, who seemed nice enough. She left fairly quickly to help Adam with dinner downstairs, though, and the girls were alone with each other and their thoughts for the first time in hours. Hannah collapsed on one of the two twin beds, the one closer to the door. Jiao Ming had offered hers to Isla, but Isla insisted she didn't mind sleeping on the cot Adam had brought up.

Isla placed her bag on her temporary blanket and went to sit beside Hannah. "How are you doing?"

What a question. "I don't know," Hannah said. "None of this feels real still." Her parents almost felt distant now, like they hadn't even been real in the first place. She wondered if that would change. Part of her hoped it would, while the other part desperately clung to the unreality of it all.

"Yeah." Isla lay beside her sister, who shifted slightly to make room. "Thank you. For getting me out."

Hannah gripped Isla's hand. "I had to," she said. "You're my sister."

After only a short while on the road, not even a full day, Hannah felt as though she'd been traveling for half her life. That evening, at the safe house, she was so preoccupied with her dinner that she didn't even register Morgan and Shane join them until Shane sat directly in front of her. She looked up into his bleary eyes, and he cracked a small smile, likely for her benefit.

"Sleep well?" Adam passed Shane and Morgan plates. They both murmured their thanks, and Adam said, "Jiao Ming and I were talking before dinner. We'll leave in two days. So rest tomorrow, and then we head out before first light."

Hannah swallowed hard. She supposed it was for the best that they move on. She would sure miss the privilege of not foraging, though. Her pack, unlike Morgan's, contained not food, but her iPhone, off of course, and her pink penguin key chain that her best friend Yara had given her. It was tucked away in the back so it wouldn't make noise. Not even Isla knew she had it. Hannah was already hyperaware of being the youngest person in the group and didn't want anyone thinking she was too sentimental or something.

She would give up her phone if she had to. But the thought of giving up her key chain made her want to cry.

"That's good," Morgan said.

"We'll travel during the day. We'll take hammocks and pretend to be campers if we're caught. Hopefully we won't be, but if we are, we better hope we're far away from here."

"Just the six of us?"

"And my friend Zoe," Adam said. "I think you've met

before? She's been transporting refugees, too, and people are starting to get suspicious. Time to go."

"Ok. I trust you."

Hannah glanced over at Isla, who was hanging on Adam's every word. Hannah didn't know Adam Boeck from a hole in the wall, but Morgan trusted him, and Isla trusted Morgan. That would have to be enough for now.

*　*　*

Zoe Ivanova wasn't happy to be traveling with a group of seven, and even less happy to learn that two of them were practically children. But she had two things in common with Morgan Young, even if she didn't know it yet: Both of them trusted Adam Boeck, and both of them knew that doing this work wasn't a choice for them.

The others met Zoe in Adam's driveway with backpacks full of canned goods and a change of clothes. She, Adam, and Morgan all carried handguns. Shane carried basic medical supplies, like bandages and pain killers.

"Everyone, this is Zoe." Adam gestured to their newest companion, who gave them a small, sardonic salute. The others mumbled their welcome.

"Alright, Adam will be in front, me in back, the rest of you in the middle. We don't want anyone getting lost in the dark." Zoe's eyes fell on Hannah, the youngest. Hannah glanced back up at Zoe with a defiant stare.

Good. Zoe hoped that meant she'd be able to handle this.

*　*　*

Morgan opened her mouth to say that she, too, could lead, and then closed it again. She didn't come to Adam as a revolutionary, but as a refugee, and her first priority had to be herself, her husband, and the two kids she dragged into this whole mess. Against her every instinct, she kept quiet.

Out of the corner of her eye, Morgan saw Shane frown at her. Had he seen her move to speak? She shook her head, a small, imperceptible gesture to anyone except for the man who had known and loved her for more than twenty years.

He came up beside her as they began to walk. "What's wrong?"

Morgan took his hand. "Just stay with me."

*   *   *

It took all the energy Hannah had not to cry. It hadn't fully hit her until then, the gravity of what happened. Her parents were dead. She was both a refugee and a fugitive from the law. She would likely never see her home again. She hated that the last one affected her so much—a house was just four walls and a roof, right?—but it did. There was an emptiness inside her when she thought about her room with the blue wallpaper and the potted plants in the window, the double swing on the front porch, the cranberry-colored couch her mother loved. It was as though something inside her was gone, a hole left in its wake.

"How's everyone doing back there?" Adam called over his shoulder. There was a "fine" from Jiao Ming and an "ok" from Shane. Otherwise, silence.

They arrived at a small clearing nearly indistinguishable to Hannah from the other spots they'd passed. Adam found it suitable, though, so he stopped there and dropped his pack to the ground. The sun was setting quickly, leaving the night cold and bitter.

"Let me know if you need help setting up your hammocks," he said. And the others got to work.

*　*　*

Zoe was setting up her own hammock when Jiao Ming approached her. "I just wanted to thank you," Jiao Ming said. "For taking charge."

Zoe kept her back turned. "Yup."

A pause, and then Jiao Ming tried again. "How'd you get started, you know . . . ?"

Zoe sighed and crossed her arms, finally looking at Jiao Ming. "Why don't you help the kids with their hammocks?"

"Oh, um, ok." Zoe heard rather than saw Jiao Ming leave and resisted the urge to look back as she tied her hammock to the second tree. She wasn't here to make friends. She wasn't here to make small talk. And she most definitely wasn't here to accept praise for nearly getting caught by the Militum.

Chapter Six

Christian Shore made it back to Virginia just after midnight, but headquarters still bustled with activity. He passed officers dragging domestic terrorists, some confirmed, some suspected, into cells. Officers chatted in the hall by the water cooler. He walked down to the last office, the name Jackson Shore in peeling silver letters on the door. He turned the knob and walked right in.

His father's office was relatively sparse, with white walls and a grey, linoleum floor. The mahogany desk, the two leather desk chairs on either side, and a metal filing cabinet was the only furniture in the room. Jackson, flanked by his degrees that hung framed above the fireplace, put a finger in the air, his ear against his phone. He was technically off duty, but he still wore his black captain's uniform. "Huh. Alright. Thanks, Joseph." He put the phone facedown on his desk and studied his visitor. "What can I do for you, Son?"

"Why did you ask me back here?" Chris demanded. "I know the prisoners escaped, but I did everything in my power to—"

"I know."

"It was the sister—"

"I know that, too."

"So then why did you ask me back here?" Chris was fuming

now, cheeks blazing red, leaning over his father's desk.

Jackson stood slowly, not looking at Chris. When he finally did, his eyebrows furrowed over his blue eyes and his mouth formed a tight line. He said, "You've grossly misread the situation, Chris."

Misread? Chris blinked and took a step back. "I don't understand."

"I didn't bring you back here to berate you," Jackson said. "I brought you back here to give you a promotion."

"Oh." Chris hid his hands behind his back and cleared his throat. "I see."

"We can talk about it in the morning, alright?" Jackson gestured toward the door. Chris blinked, then exited the way he came, but with much less anger.

* * *

The door closed, and Jackson sighed. He sat again, resting his elbows on the desk and bringing his fingers together. Christian would make a fine sergeant. He was young, sure. But from two years old, since the time of his adoption, Jackson raised him to be an enforcer of the law.

Despite the late hour, Jackson turned on his computer. The promotion was about Christian's strength as an officer, sure, but more, he knew the boy thrived with encouragement, that he would stop at nothing if someone just believed in him.

And Jackson desperately needed him to get those prisoners back.

* * *

Even as a young boy, Christian was desperate to be a captain one day. He used to sneak into his father's closet when he was sure he wouldn't be caught, at least, mostly sure, and study his father's silken blue uniforms and his badge. He placed his small hands over its cool metal and over the lapels of the uniform, and imagined it was his.

He entered the academy just out of high school. Right away, he felt different from the other boys for a multitude of reasons.

One, he already knew most of what they were supposed to be learning, even compared to the other kids who grew up with officer parents. He tried to hide it from the others, but far too often, their instructors would single him out to answer questions no one else wanted to touch or ask him to demonstrate a skill they weren't supposed to know.

Two, of the one hundred students in the academy, Chris was one of three people of color and the only Black kid. And because of his lightish-dark skin and green eyes, many of the others felt entitled to ask what he was, as if he were an alien species and possibly dangerous. The only time he interacted with someone who looked like him was when he stayed late enough to see the cleaning crew or caught a glimpse of the lunch staff.

Three, his reasoning for being there suddenly felt off when he listened to the others in his year talk about their drive, their dedication to their country, their duty to their fellow Americans. And even though there were other boys who wanted to follow in their parents' footsteps, Christian suddenly felt that his determination to make his father proud rang hollow. Six years later, it still did.

* * *

Every night, Hannah screamed in her sleep. Zoe saw Shane's eyes flutter open and Adam place his hands over his ears, but no one said a word. She suspected none of them said anything because they, like her, didn't want to embarrass Hannah more than she was surely already embarrassed.

After six nights of this, Zoe decided it was time to act. They'd been walking for three hours when Zoe approached Morgan. "Switch with me," she said.

"Oh. Ok . . ." Morgan fell back, and Shane stayed with her, letting Isla and Jiao Ming pass them. Assuring herself that Morgan was in position to protect the group from the back, Zoe moved ahead.

She caught up with Hannah, who was walking behind Adam, her shoulders hunched and her head down. "Hey."

Hannah blinked up at her. "Are you talking to me?"

Ouch, but fair. Zoe hadn't exactly been social. "I heard Isla tell Morgan that you're pretty good at stars," Zoe said, ignoring that last question, still unsure whether it was a deliberate dig or genuine confusion. "Can you teach me?"

"Teach you? Like, constellations and stuff?" Zoe nodded. "Yeah, tonight I can show you some of the basic ones."

"Cool." Zoe paused, realizing she had nothing else to say to Hannah. "Um, great." She headed to the back of the line and wordlessly slipped behind Morgan.

Zoe watched as Hannah's shoulders straightened, as the girl began to smile for the first time since Zoe had met her. It made Hannah look so young, like she really was sixteen. Hannah pointed up at the sky. "Well, that's the Big Dipper," she said. "See how it kind of looks like a spoon?"

Zoe saw nothing but a cluster of bright dots. "I think so,"

she said.

"And then the Little Dipper next to it." Using her finger, Hannah traced something in the air that only she could see. "Next to them are," Hannah continued as Zoe turned to find Jiao Ming watching them. She thought she caught Jiao Ming watching her every once in a while or maybe more than that, and for some reason, the thought made her dizzy. She tried to refocus on Hannah, who appeared to be in her own world.

Eventually, Jiao Ming turned in, and Hannah did, too. Zoe stayed up for a bit longer, listening for the screams, but they never came. For the first time in a week, Hannah slept through the night.

Isla fell back on the next day's walk until she was side by side with Zoe. "Thank you."

Zoe raised her eyebrows. "For?"

"Talking to Hannah." Isla gestured to her sister, who was talking animatedly with Shane. "She's like a different person."

"She just needed a distraction. It's really not a big deal."

"Still. Thank you." Isla left, and Zoe's gaze fell on Jiao Ming. Was she watching her?

Jiao Ming turned back sharply, nearly tripping over a tree root. Zoe snorted, and Jiao Ming glanced at her shyly. They exchanged small smiles, and Zoe quickly looked away.

*　*　*

That evening, Shane sat with Hannah to talk medicine, so Morgan took up residence at Adam's side. "Anything I can do?" she asked.

Adam shook his head. "Not at the moment." He had set up his own hammock and was tending to their fire. Morgan frowned, and Adam quickly added, "We'll need food later, though, if you want to get hunting."

"Yeah, that would be good." She was quiet for a moment, thinking. She was unused to being the one who needed help; she always did the helping. She didn't like the feeling.

"Remember when you and I took a group to California together, maybe six or seven years ago?"

"With the little girl," Morgan said. "I remember."

"You were so patient with her. I'd never have that kind of patience."

Morgan cracked a half smile. He could tell she was upset. Of course he could. "You're just saying that."

"I'm not. I'm sorry it's come to this, Morgan."

She met his eyes, wide and solemn. He meant it. So she just nodded and said, "Thank you." She left him, thinking.

As she set up her hammock, she thought about that little girl. Melina, Morgan recalled. She and her father fled after the father, a former journalist, had been discovered running an underground newspaper. The girl was perhaps five at the time, and yet she was already resigned. It was Morgan's first and only time transporting such a young refugee to California. Where might she be now? She never knew what happened after her charges crossed into California. Perhaps someone at Border Brothers, the group that helped refugees settle in California, would know.

Morgan finished her temporary bed and sat on the edge, massaging her knee with both hands. Shane shot her a look of concern, but before he could say anything, Isla approached. "Ms. Y—Morgan?"

Morgan smiled slightly at the slipup. She couldn't imagine the way Isla must view her now, knowing the whole story. But it was nice in some ways to know that Isla still viewed her as her teacher, someone she respected. "What's up?" She gestured for Isla to sit next to her.

"I was just wondering," Isla said, taking a seat, "is this the way you always go? When you take people to California."

Morgan shrugged. "Sometimes. We change it up, so no one catches on and follows us."

"Oh. That makes sense."

"Have you ever been camping before?" Morgan asked. "Not that this is exactly family fun time."

"Yeah. Hannah and I have been before with our parents. At Bullfrog Lake mostly."

"We've been there," Shane said, indicating himself and Morgan. "It's beautiful."

"Did you make s'mores and all that?" Morgan asked.

Isla's eyes lit up for a moment. "Of course. My dad and Hannah made a fire, and we all sat around it. And then Hannah mostly ate the chocolate and marshmallows without the crackers." Isla stopped suddenly, her lips pressed together, and Morgan didn't push her. The light had gone out.

Morgan couldn't imagine what must be behind that young, haunted gaze. Isla would never see her parents again. She'd probably never go back to Bullfrog Lake. At last, Isla said, "You fought. Both of you," she added, acknowledging Shane. "In the war. Was it required? Because my parents didn't."

"No. It wasn't required."

"Then why did you?"

"It depended. For me, it was what was right. My parents

were incensed, to say the least. My mother screamed at me not to go."

"Did they support Powers?"

Morgan's eyes narrowed. "They didn't support much of anything, really." She left it at that.

Shane sat on his own hammock across from them. "I went because they paid for school," he said. "My family supported the effort, but really I went because we were broke. And then we lost, so it was . . . I mean, it wasn't for nothing. But I had to pay my own way."

"You fought?" Jiao Ming asked. She was standing by the tree at the foot of Shane's temporary bed. "Both of you?"

"I was a medic," Shane told her.

"In the same unit?"

"Yes. That's how we met."

Morgan gave him a small smile across the clearing. Everything went wrong after she enlisted. Except meeting Shane. She felt a rush of gratitude for him, for his love.

She turned to Jiao Ming. "What brought you here?"

Jiao Ming shrugged. "I'm DACA, you know? My parents brought me over from China as a kid and, well, a colleague ratted me out." Behind them, Zoe turned to listen from her own hammock.

They all sat with that for a moment. "So . . . you're undocumented?" Isla finally asked.

"Sort of. DACA is Deferred Action for Childhood Arrivals. So I was never a citizen, but I was allowed to be here. Until they took DACA away."

"I'm sorry," Morgan offered.

"Being displaced just kind of sucks," she said. "And it

doesn't get any easier."

The silence resumed for a moment, each member of the group in their own thoughts. At last, Zoe said, "That's brave. To keep going."

Jiao Ming looked over at Zoe, her knees tucked up to her chest and her arms around her legs. Morgan watched the gaze intensify between them. She knew that look. At last, Jiao Ming nodded. "Thank you," she said.

Morgan stretched, lying down behind Isla with her leg extended. "It's late," she said. "We have a long way to walk in the morning." Long, she thought, and painful in more ways than one.

Jiao Ming nodded. "Goodnight." She left with Isla, and Zoe lay down in her hammock. As the rest of the group took their leave, Shane sat in Isla's spot.

"You ok?" he asked Morgan.

"Just tired." Her hand found his and squeezed.

"Ok." He bent over and kissed her on the lips, featherlight.

Morgan closed her eyes then and felt rather than saw Shane's hand slip away. That was ok, though. She knew he'd be right there when she woke up.

Chapter Seven

In her anxiety about the day ahead, Hannah got up before the others. She slipped away, back to a clearing she remembered passing not far from camp, hoping to see the last of the stars as the sun began to slip over the horizon.

Among the sounds of the cicadas singing and the twittering birds just beginning to wake up, Hannah heard another sound: a human voice. She frowned and listened carefully. It was a deeper voice, but not Shane-deep. Adam, maybe? She went ahead, keeping close to the trees.

Hannah wasn't entirely sure why she was sneaking along when she and Adam were on the same team, but she continued to do so until she could hear the words clearly: "A few days . . . no, that shouldn't be a problem . . . remember, I told you about the injury. It's definitely . . . oh, yes, of course. Not a problem, Sir. Take care."

Carefully, Hannah peered around the oak tree. Adam was on a cell phone? But he and Zoe both told them not to bring theirs. Could he keep his because he wasn't being hunted?

Adam moved past Hannah, and she skirted around her tree, heart pounding. It was probably nothing, she told herself. She didn't want Isla to worry about her. She was still the youngest, still the girl who'd woken up screaming in the night. And she wanted desperately to be able to do this.

*   *   *

Isla stared out at the vast expanse of highway before them. Cars zipped by so quickly they wouldn't have seen the travelers even if they weren't still half in the forest. "Are you sure this is the only way?" Shane whispered beside her.

"Unless you want to add another two weeks," Adam said. They retreated deeper into the forest, where Adam pulled a map from his pack and flattened it on the ground. Their trail was already marked in dark green sharpie. Isla tried to visualize the old map in Morgan's classroom. They were almost in Kansas, but she wasn't sure exactly what that looked like on the old map. California was bigger on this one, though, and the edge of it marked the end of their trail. Before history that year, Isla had only thought of California as the state that split off from the U.S. She never really interrogated why the state seceded.

Morgan frowned as she studied the map. "Won't we look suspicious traveling all together?"

"We won't," Adam said, "because we won't be traveling together. I'll go first with Jiao Ming, then Shane, Isla, and Hannah will go, then you and Zoe."

Isla's heart dropped into her stomach.

"No," Morgan argued, her face suddenly pale. "Absolutely not."

"It's the best way."

"I'm not sending them without a guide."

"We'll only be ten minutes apart. You'll be on them before anything happens."

Her heart pounded, but she didn't say anything else. She thought Adam was right about needing to go in smaller groups. That didn't mean she hated it any less. And it didn't mean she thought this was the right way.

"How will we know where to go?" Shane asked. "There's only one map."

"You'll take it," Adam said. "Zoe and I both know where to go." Morgan appeared to be fighting tears. Shane put a hand on her shoulder, and Adam looked away. Isla struggled to find any words to describe her sinking terror and came up empty.

Zoe snorted and finally said what Isla was thinking. "So you're assuming Shane, Isla, and Hannah will be less conspicuous traveling together because they're all Black?"

"I'm being pragmatic, Zo. People are less likely to remember three people the same race traveling together than an Asian woman, a white woman, and a Black man."

"What happens if they're stopped?" Jiao Ming asked. She didn't clarify, but she didn't need to. Isla had seen Black bodies on the news, and she saw the Militum justify their deaths. She knew that she, Hannah, and Shane would be in the most danger if they came into contact with an officer, and that Zoe and Morgan would be in the least.

"We'll be ok," Isla said, sounding braver than she felt. Really, she wanted to scream.

"Alright." Adam folded up the map and handed it to Shane, whose grip on Morgan's shoulder was visibly tightening. Adam stood. "We'll be walking mostly on backroads, through towns. Just talk to each other and try not to call attention to yourselves." He glanced at Jiao Ming. "You ready?"

"Yes." Jiao Ming locked eyes with Shane, and Isla wondered how the hell he was supposed to act casual while holding a map that could give them all away.

*   *   *

Shane fingered the map in his pocket, both wanting to double check their position and knowing that doing so would be a horrible idea. They were walking through a small town comprised of little shops and pedestrians who seemed to look right through them as they passed. So far, so good.

They'd established their backstory while still walking on the highway. If anyone asked, Shane was Isla and Hannah's father, and they were here on the girls' spring break, which Isla assured him would be about now. They also desperately hoped no one would ask.

"So. Um. What subjects do you like?" Shane asked, cringing internally. He was an introvert by nature and had little experience talking to teenage girls, even particularly bright teenage girls like Isla and Hannah.

Still, Isla didn't seem to mind his awkwardness. "History, a lot. English. And art. But honestly, it was hard to be in those classes. Those last two. I didn't really have friends, and the teachers always seemed to know I was different. I was always afraid of being outed."

"Oh." What did he say to that? "That couldn't have been easy."

Isla shrugged. "It's ok."

"No, it's not."

She hesitated. "No. But what can I do about it?"

"Shane!" Hannah hissed. Shane looked over at her, then at the Militum officer who was heading over.

*   *   *

As they made their way into town, people meandering in and out of the brick buildings on either side, the silence between them became palpable and heavy. Zoe hadn't spoken much to Morgan on this trip. She knew that wasn't fair. Morgan, too, had been chased from her home. At last, Zoe supplied a peace offering: a story in case they were caught by the Militum. "I could be your sister," Zoe said.

"I appreciate the thought," Morgan laughed. "But I'm way too old to be your sister."

Zoe crossed her arms. "Well, you're too young to be my mother."

"Cousins?" Morgan suggested. "Or maybe just friends. We don't really look related, besides."

"Yeah, well, Shane doesn't look like he could be related to Isla and Hannah, and yet, here we are." Zoe kicked a rock forward as they rounded a turn, nearly running into a pedestrian. The woman excused herself and continued on.

Zoe tried again. "So, the girls were your students?"

"Just Isla," Morgan said.

"And . . . you taught history, right?"

"Real history," Morgan said with a smirk.

Zoe smirked back. "Sounds rebellious."

"What did you do?"

"I just worked at an auto shop. It wasn't like a passion project or anything. Just a job. It pays the bills for school. Or it did."

"What did you study?"

"Political science," Zoe said, rolling her eyes. "Freaking useless now."

They lapsed into silence again, and Zoe found her mind wandering over to Jiao Ming. After that first night, she had started watching the other woman carefully, still somewhat wary. But Jiao Ming was brave and smart and willing to question Adam, which was always a plus to Zoe. She felt a little guilty now about how she'd shunted Jiao Ming off to the side at first. Maybe Zoe could at least be a little nicer.

"Oh, fuck." Morgan's voice snapped Zoe out of her reverie. She realized immediately what was wrong. Up ahead Shane and the girls were speaking with a Militum officer who had his hand on the gun in his holster.

* * *

"Everything ok over here?" the officer asked.

"Yes, sir," Shane said, putting his hands on the girls' shoulders. "We're fine."

The officer glanced at Hannah, then back at Shane. "I don't recognize you."

Shane's mind ran through the most likely scenarios: They go to jail when they can't answer any questions. The officer somehow recognizes them, and they're taken back to Evanston. Or they're shot on the spot. "We're just visiting," Shane told him. "It's my girls' spring break."

"Is that so?"

"Yes, sir," Shane said. Hannah grimaced as he dug his nails into her shoulder blade.

"Well, Mister?"

"Odom. Derrick Odom."

"Mr. Odom, I need to see some ID."

Shane's face fell. He was starting to answer when a voice came from behind him.

"Excuse me, sir? Officer?" Shane whipped around. Morgan came up to the group, pulling Zoe by the hand. "Could you help us? My friend and me are a little lost."

"Of course, ma'am." The officer stepped away from Shane and toward the two women. She never looked at him directly, but with a nearly imperceptible nod from Morgan, Shane knew to grab both girls and get the hell away.

*   *   *

Adam and Jiao Ming sat in the clearing, getting more nervous as the seconds ticked past and the others didn't arrive. At last, Isla and the others made it. "What took you so long?" Adam asked, both he and Jiao Ming rising from their seats on a mossy log.

"We ran into an officer," Hannah mumbled.

Jiao Ming stepped forward. "Are you ok?" she asked. Isla and Hannah both shrugged. Shane just stared at the ground. He hadn't said a word since the run-in with the man in a Militum uniform.

Another five minutes and Morgan and Zoe stomped into the clearing, both radiating fury. Morgan practically ran to Shane's side as Zoe marched up to Adam. "We told you," Zoe seethed, standing mere inches from his face. "We said we shouldn't be separated. Not like this. This is exactly what we thought could happen."

"Everyone is ok," Adam said. "We're all ok."

"But some of us might not be next time," Morgan said, squeezing Shane's shoulder. "We can't have a next time. We can't send three people out on their own without a guide when the Militum—"

"All of them are perfectly competent."

"That's not what I meant, and you fucking know it."

"Stop." Everyone looked at Isla, whose fists were clenched tightly at her sides. "We're not fine. Today sucked. I hated feeling that helpless, and I hated being saved." She rounded on Adam. "You said you would help us. So do that."

A pause. Adam stared at the ground. Zoe was practically panting with anger. Finally Isla said, "It's almost dark. Let's find a place to set up camp." She began to walk deeper into the woods, followed by the others. First Hannah, who quickly caught up to her sister, then Adam, who bowed his head forward. Shane and Morgan went next, hand in hand, him whispering something to her that no one else could hear, leaving Jiao Ming in the back with Zoe.

* * *

As they set up camp that night, Zoe approached Jiao Ming, who was rearranging her pack. "So, uh, everything go ok with you guys?"

Jiao Ming blinked twice, a spare T-shirt in her hand. "Oh. Yeah. Everything went ok."

"Cool." Zoe cringed at her own speech. Cool? Really? What was wrong with her?

Luckily, Jiao Ming didn't seem to notice. "I'm glad everyone is ok," she said, rising.

"Me too." Zoe locked eyes with Jiao Ming, then quickly

looked away.

"You're, um, a good leader," Jiao Ming said. "You're doing a good job." Her face flushed, but Zoe, still looking at the ground, didn't notice.

"Thanks," she said, and she bit her lip to stop herself from grinning. She wasn't sure she was a leader in this case, needing to flee the country herself. But she couldn't deny she was glad Jiao Ming thought so.

*　　*　　*

Jackson and his team could have met up with Adam and the others at the end of the trail, it's true. Jackson knew Christian was wondering why they didn't do just that. But Christian didn't know that Jackson planned on taking out any help this group happened to have on their way to California. A necessary evil if they wanted to cut the rebels off from any help, both domestic and international.

And Christian didn't have to know that, yet. Though his son was now a sergeant, Jackson still wanted to protect him in a way.

Besides, it was good to go out on the trail. What if Boeck betrayed them somehow, even after promising to help the Militum? What if the group began to suspect something was amiss and slipped away? Jackson needed to stay on top of it.

Jackson remembered how Boeck shook when Jackson himself had arrived at his door the previous winter. How, when he whispered subtle threats of torture in Adam's ear and went to cuff his hands, Adam broke down and promised to do whatever the other man wanted. Including betraying his colleagues. Including becoming a spy.

So Jackson pressed forward with his men. They had to capture these rebels who made such a fool of him and the regime. He would not be made a fool of. He had come too far.

That evening, standing beside his father as a sergeant, unaware that their next stop would mean the end of a man's life, Christian felt a heaviness in his chest, the weight of the seriousness of his position. He would serve it well. He, too, had come too far not to.

Jackson called out to the officers. "Alright men, Boeck's group was planning on stopping here." He pointed to a spot on the map. "We'll be stopping here for the evening." He pointed to the spot that represented their camp, several miles behind Adam and the others.

The crew began to set up tents between the trees. As Jackson suspected, Christian really didn't get the point of familiarizing themselves with the trail when they could just take a flight to the final rendezvous point and be done with it. But of course, he didn't say anything.

He was a soldier, and he would obey his commander.

<u>Chapter Eight</u>

The seven of them gathered around the entry before they went into the pharmacy that night. Adam started, "Arnie says there shouldn't be anyone there but him right now, but you never know, so—"

"We get it," Zoe said, arms crossed. "Code names, we don't know each other, blah, blah, blah."

"This is serious."

"And we can handle it."

Adam glared at her for a moment longer and then relented. "Fine," he said. "Let's go."

They turned toward the pharmacy, opened the door, and blinked as their eyes adjusted to the bright, artificial lights. Zoe took one last look out the back, just to make sure they weren't being followed, and then let the door swing shut behind them.

Arnie greeted them at the counter. "It's good to see you, Adam," he said, nodding in his direction. "Zoe," he said, with a nod in hers.

Adam shook his hand. "Thanks, Arnie. We'll be quick."

Arnie waved a hand. "Take your time. I never get anyone in here between three and four o'clock in the morning."

Shane immediately went to the medical supply aisle

while Morgan asked Arnie if he happened to have any ammo for their guns. Isla and Hannah drifted over to the canned goods. Adam peered out the back door again, just in case.

No one noticed Zoe, and that was fine by her. Carefully, she crept into the back room and began her search.

C'mon, c'mon. Surely someone called in a prescription for somethi—Got it! Zoe grabbed two rather large bottles of Protridon and went to stuff them in her bag.

"Zoe?"

She jumped, smacking her head and sending its contents flying. "Fuck!" Zoe rubbed her head and glared at Jiao Ming, who was stifling either a laugh or a yelp. "What?" Somehow, she realized, in her scramble to find drugs, she'd forgotten about Jiao Ming. Zoe quickly stuffed the Pro in her bag and tried to look casual. Well, casually angry.

"I was just checking to see if there's anything useful. You know, back here."

"Oh. Yeah. Same."

Jiao Ming frowned and eyed the bag in Zoe's hand. "Are you sure?"

Zoe narrowed her eyes. "Are you accusing me of something?"

"Zoe, we're on the same side."

"That doesn't answer my question." She cursed herself for saying anything. It would be better not to pick a fight, wouldn't it? That, and a small part of Zoe was mad at herself for not just being angry, but for being angry at Jiao Ming.

"I'm not accusing you of anything." Jiao Ming crossed her arms and took a step back. For a brief moment, Zoe wanted to tell her everything. Something screamed in her mind that she could trust this woman and that she should. Instead, she pushed past Jiao Ming and left.

Zoe moaned with pleasure as she swallowed the Pro she'd snuck moments after they'd set up camp. It wasn't like she was an addict or anything. Every once in a while though, she needed to escape from her own brain.

After her ex-girlfriend, Aviva, was taken away, after her parents kicked her out, she stayed with a series of friends until she found a job willing to take on a scrawny, teenage girl with no experience and no references while she could finish high school online. She moved to Falletville and stayed with a woman named Leigh, who spent most of her time high on Pro. Zoe broke up with her and got her own place after six months, but she was already hooked on the drug.

Before Aviva was arrested, they were sixteen and completely in love, though Zoe wouldn't have called it that. She maintained she couldn't know what love was at such a young age, especially with a woman, but Aviva undoubtedly made her feel something she had never felt before. A something that made her heart drop into her stomach and her head swim with visions of their future together. Late one night, after Aviva's parents left on a work trip for her father, they lay wrapped up in each other, Aviva's arms around Zoe's shoulders. "Let's stay like this forever," Aviva breathed into Zoe's hair.

"Mmm. What about when your parents get home?"

"We'll stop time. They'll never come home."

"Mmm. Very realistic."

"Zo?" Zoe turned her face up to Aviva, who was suddenly serious. "I'd do anything for you. You know that?"

Zoe nodded. "Yeah," she said. "Me too." It was a scary feeling, to want to protect someone she knew she was putting in danger every day. But it was a feeling she knew to be true all the same. She kissed Aviva gently, then harder, rotating her body so that she was on top.

The snap of a twig brought Zoe back into the clearing. She whipped around and saw Jiao Ming, clearly looking to bolt.

Zoe strode forward and grabbed Jiao Ming's arm. "What the fuck? Did you follow me?"

"No!" Jiao Ming held up her hands in surrender, knocking Zoe's hand away. "Well, yes. Adam asked me to make sure you were ok."

"Well, I'm fine."

"I, um, I saw the Pro," she said. "I don't want to pretend I didn't."

Zoe flushed. "I'm not walking around high all the time, jeez. Why do you even care?"

Jiao Ming's eyes went wide, and she blushed fiercely. Suddenly, Zoe realized how close they were standing. So close she was sure Jiao Ming could see every freckle across her nose, every near-translucent eyelash. "Oh."

"Forget it," Jiao Ming said. Her eyes sparkled, and she took a step back, leaving Zoe cold without the extra body heat. So Zoe grabbed her arm.

Jiao Ming frowned. "What are you doing?"

Zoe didn't answer. Honestly, she wasn't sure how she felt about Jiao Ming, other than good. But maybe that was enough. She put her hands on either side of Jiao Ming's face and kissed her.

For a moment, Jiao Ming's lips were stiff, unresponsive. Then she kissed Zoe back. Zoe let her hands travel down Jiao Ming's side and back up again, humming contentedly. She spun them both and pushed Jiao Ming back against a tree. "Wait."

Zoe stopped, breathing hard. "Are you . . . is this ok?"

Jiao Ming was shaking. "This . . . this will mean a lot more to me than it will to you."

"What do you mean?"

"I actually like you, Zoe. You know, as a person." Jiao Ming bit her lip, letting the silence linger.

"And you think I don't like you?" Zoe asked. Her hand was on Jiao Ming's hip again, tracing gentle circles over her clothes. "Do you know how stupid that sounds?"

"Excuse me?"

"You're funny," Zoe said. "And you're brave. And . . . yeah, I like you, you fucking jerk." She smiled when she said it, though, and Jiao Ming smiled back at her. "Oh."

Zoe laughed. "Yeah. Oh." Zoe took a small step back. "So, um . . ."

Jiao Ming stepped forward this time and took both of Zoe's hands in hers as their lips met.

* * *

They were making surprisingly good time, so Adam said, "Let's take a day off."

Zoe nearly dropped the ends of her hammock. "I'm sorry, are you insane? The faster we get there—"

"I know, but we shouldn't wear ourselves out, right?" The sun was just beginning to set, illuminating them all from behind. "Morgan, what do you think?"

Morgan hesitated. "I . . . it doesn't matter what I think."

"Don't say that," Adam protested. "I care what you think."

She sighed. Really, her knee was beginning to bug her again, and she was dying for a day with just Shane, just a little bit of time alone. But was that selfish? She had to get Isla and Hannah to safety. But Hannah just looked so tired.

"One day," she agreed. "That's it." As she said the words, she saw Isla sag a bit in relief. Hannah tried to hide her small, tired smile, and Morgan knew she had made the right choice.

Zoe glared. "Fine. But if we get caught, I'm blaming you idiots."

Adam ignored her and stifled a yawn. "Alright, I'm turning in. Come daytime, do what you'd like. Just stay close."

The others nodded and returned to setting up their supplies. Adam bit his lip and looked over at Morgan, who was putting up her hammock next to Shane's.

*   *   *

Hannah waited until she was almost sure everyone was asleep before sneaking off to the clearing they'd passed less than a mile back. She understood why they slept in places where the trees were thicker and the branches obstructed aerial views. Really, she did. But she still missed the stars.

As children, Hannah and Isla both had glow-in-the-dark star sets that their father offered to stick on their ceilings. Isla just let hers sit on her bookshelf until she lost track of them, but Hannah and her father spent an unforgettable afternoon putting her stars up in the shapes of constellations and spacing out the planets, so they were the proper distance from the sun. To scale, of course.

Back in the clearing, Hannah lay down on the grass and

examined the sky. She could see Ursa Major, and—

"You shouldn't sneak off like that." Hannah jerked upright and whipped around, but it was only Zoe. Hannah exhaled through her nose and lay back on the grass.

"And you shouldn't follow people, so you can sneak up on them."

Zoe sat beside her. "Fair." She lay back, head-to-feet with Hannah. "What are we looking at?"

"Ursa Major is that one." Hannah pointed to the stars and drew an outline with her finger. "And Ursa Minor." She shifted her hand and made a similar motion. "They're bears." Neither of them said anything for a moment. Then Hannah broke the silence and said, "My dad taught me all this. He was a scientist. He studied space."

"Adam told me what happened to your parents. I'm sorry."

Hannah didn't know what to say to that. Shane or Morgan must have said something to Adam. Probably Morgan. It shouldn't bother her, but there was something about Adam she just didn't trust, which was probably unfair. She remembered overhearing him on the phone and felt uneasy, but she pushed the feeling aside.

"Do you have any family?" Hannah finally asked. "People you're leaving behind?"

"Nope. My darling parents kicked me out when I told them I like women. And my sisters haven't spoken to me since."

Hannah made a face. She couldn't imagine what that must be like, especially after seeing her parents take such care to make Isla feel like her womanhood was valid, even if they didn't understand it. "Damn."

She felt Zoe shrug next to her. "Doesn't matter," Zoe said. She sat up then and stood. "Come back soon, ok?"

"Sure." Hannah listened to Zoe's footsteps until all she could hear was the wind blowing through the trees, a distant owl, and the sound of her own heart.

* * *

Shane woke to the first rays of the day's light appearing over the trees. He glanced at Morgan, who lay on her back with her eyes open, staring up at the leafy canopy. "Hey," he whispered, reaching out for her hand.

She looked over at him and smiled, her mind still a bit hazy with sleep. "Hey." She bridged the gap, and their fingers brushed.

"Can you hear that?"

Morgan listened. The breeze knocked gently into the leaves overhead. Elsewhere, birds were waking and singing. And then she heard it.

"Water." Somewhere close a running stream.

"Let's go find it?"

Morgan slipped out of her hammock and hissed as her left foot hit the ground, radiating white-hot pain from her knee out. Her old injury had caused her knee to swell in the night and it made it difficult for her to put pressure on her left leg.

"Morgan?" Shane came up behind her and put his hand on her back.

"It's just my knee," she said. "I'm fine."

Shane narrowed his eyes but didn't say anything. The two of them made their way down to the river together slowly, and with much help from Shane in Morgan's case. She sat on a rock beside the running water, unlaced her shoes, and rolled up her pant leg. She lowered her left leg into the water until it covered her knee, tears springing into her eyes as the swollen scar tissue fully submerged.

She hated being helpless like this. It recalled other, darker, moments of despair. Her shoulders tensed at the feelings that washed through her. Biting pain in her stomach and a debilitating horror. The breath of her fellow soldier on her neck. The lightning-illuminated shape of a man.

"You shouldn't be walking on it," Shane said, sitting beside her on the rock.

Morgan shook the memory away and bit back a snappy retort. "I don't exactly have a choice."

"You could ride on my back," he offered. "Or we can make crutches, somehow."

"We'd slow them down."

"So we split up. We can tell them—"

"No."

"Morgan—"

"Isla and Hannah are only here because of me," she hissed. "I'm not leaving them, and I'm not slowing them down."

Her head dropped onto Shane's shoulder, and he shifted so that his arm wrapped securely around her. "You can't blame yourself."

"I should have realized. Why do you think they took Isla? She's not the only student I've ever gotten close with. They took her because she's a trans, Black girl, and I gave them an excuse." She practically spat the last few words, as though they were bitter on her tongue. "I should have known. I should have—"

"Morgan, stop." She did stop, breathing hard. "If you could stop this from happening, if you could trade all you've done for the revolution to stop them from coming for us, would you do it?" Shane asked.

They both knew the answer really. But it was different saying it. And hearing it. So she said, "No. I wouldn't."

"So no more guilt," Shane said. "It won't help Isla. It won't help us get to California. And it won't help our cause." He grabbed her hand over her shoulder and squeezed. "You could at least wrap the knee."

He felt her smile against his neck. It sent shivers down his spine. But he didn't know why she was smiling. He didn't know that Morgan had noticed a subtle difference in the way he spoke of the revolution. "Our cause," he said.

"Ok," she conceded. "I'll wrap the knee."

Chapter Nine

Adam couldn't help but look behind him every few feet. Someone must have figured him out by now. Zoe and Morgan were both far too clever, and he got the feeling that Hannah Logan still didn't quite trust him.

But Adam wasn't stupid either, and he noticed Morgan near-limping for the last day or so. She was always reluctant to tell him anything about her time in the army, but when she had to take time off for one of several reconstructive surgeries, she was forced to confess her trauma. Adam suspected there was more that he didn't know about.

He didn't want to come out and ask her if she needed a break. She would never stop just for herself. But if he happened to suggest a stop at the same time she was in pain . . .

Adam sat at the edge of the water and contemplated his position. Was that awful, to take advantage of her pain like that? Or more awful than what he was already doing? He pushed the thought out of his head. Maybe he wasn't cut out for this life. But wouldn't anyone else have done the same? No. Morgan hadn't. But then, he always knew that Morgan was the better person.

Out of the trees, Shore appeared, flanked by two officers and, from what Adam could see of his uniform, a sergeant. Adam stood.

"At ease, Boeck."

Adam sat back on the rock. "Evening, Captain."

Shore gestured to the sergeant beside him. "My son, Christian." Then he motioned to the men behind him. "Officers York and Bolentio."

The younger Shore looked over at Adam, who hesitated before asking, "Have we met before?"

Christian frowned. "I don't believe so." He didn't seem to be lying, and Adam couldn't recall being introduced before, but there was something familiar about Sergeant Shore in the depths of his eyes, in the shape of his jaw.

"Were you in Evanston?"

"Yes. But I don't believe—"

"Have you made contact with your collaborators on the other side of the border?" Jackson Shore interrupted.

"Yes, Sir. They're prepared to meet us on our side in two weeks' time." Adam took a breath and forced himself calm again.

"Wonderful. And no one has any suspicions?"

A brief image of Hannah flashed through his mind, her eyes narrows and her mouth turned down in a frown. Adam banished the image from his mind. "No. Nothing."

Captain Shore clapped him on the shoulder, still standing over him. "Wonderful," he said again, and Adam felt like crying.

*   *   *

Both Hannah and Isla had fallen asleep that evening when Zoe broke out the rum in her pack. "What happened to only essentials?" Jiao Ming teased.

"Rum is essential," Zoe argued, and she sat next to Shane, who had just finished building a fire. She drank from the flask and passed it over to Shane. "We'll leave early tomorrow," Adam said, sitting down across from them.

"Yeah because we just lost a whole day," Zoe mumbled. Jiao Ming and Morgan came to sit with them. Shane watched Morgan carefully as she sat down. She appeared to be in less pain than before, but of course she would never say anything to him in front of the others. She was the strongest person he knew, but sometimes he worried she was too strong, that she would push herself to her limit and not be able to come back.

"I think we all needed a day," Adam said, looking directly at Morgan. Zoe followed his gaze and frowned. "What?" she asked.

Adam bit his lip. Finally he said, "Nothing."

"Adam, what aren't you telling us?" Zoe glanced back at Morgan, who was staring into the flames. "Morgan?"

Shane leaned toward Zoe and murmured, "Stop."

"If you two are keeping secrets—"

"I was shot." They all looked over at Morgan, who appeared to be speaking directly to the burning logs before them. Shane put a hand on her arm, offering strength. Taking it, Morgan continued, "As a soldier. Sometimes my knee flares up where the bullet went through." To Adam she said, "You knew that, and I guess you realized it was hurting. But I swear, Adam, if that's why we spent the day—" Her hands shook, and Shane moved his own hand on top of hers.

"It isn't."

Zoe shifted in her seat. "I'm sorry," she said. "I didn't know." The group fell silent. Shane passed the flask to Morgan, who took a long drink and handed it back. Shane squeezed Morgan's hand, and she turned hers over so that their palms touched.

"I am sorry," Zoe said again. "Really."

Morgan offered her a small smile. "It's ok. In your shoes, I might've asked, too."

There was a long moment of silence. Next to Shane, Morgan trembled, nearly imperceptibly. He wanted to wrap his arms around her, to tell her it was going to be ok, but she wouldn't want him to do that in front of everyone else. So he settled for lacing their fingers together more tightly.

"I have a ton of Pro in my bag," Zoe blurted. They all stared at her, and Zoe's face went bright red. "I, uh, in the interest of not keeping things from the group, you know? I, um, stole it from the pharmacy. I actually got caught doing work for our cause because one of my dealer's clients ratted me out for a plea deal." Zoe licked her lips and stared at a beetle crawling on the end of a burning log, trying to avoid everyone's gaze. "I'm not an addict. I just, it's an escape. Sometimes this"—she gestured all around her— "is just too much." Next to her, Jiao Ming shifted closer and placed a hand on her back. Shane recognized the gesture, an effort to release a small part of the tension there.

"If you ever wanted to, uh, try something else, I could help you," he offered. "Not that you wouldn't be able to do it on your own. I just, I've done it with patients before."

"No, I'm . . . thank you." Zoe forced herself to make eye contact with him. She grabbed the rum out of his hands and took another swig of it.

* * *

Sitting at the fire, Shane found part of him slipping back into the medic tent twenty years ago, watching two of Morgan's superiors half carry her into the room. Her pants were soaked through with blood, and her eyes were half closed. The bullet had gone straight through, both a blessing (no immediate surgery needed) and a curse (more blood loss). One of the men turned to Shane as he ran over. "She's bleeding pretty heavily, but it's mostly the pain. Do you have anything for her?"

He did, of course, and he yelled for another medic to get it while he staunched the blood from Morgan's wound with a cloth. She lay on one of the cots, staining the white sheets red. Every breath looked like a chore. The other medic handed Shane the medication and took his place by Morgan's knee. Shane put a hand on Morgan's arm. "Morgan? Can you hear me?"

"Y-yes." Her lips barely moved, but Shane heard her. If he wasn't treating her, he would have wept with relief. They were already inexplicably close. He already loved her, though he wouldn't admit it to even himself for several weeks.

He tilted her head back and forced her to swallow the bitter liquid. She turned her head to the side, gagging. The other medic took a step back, forcing Shane to suppress an eye roll. "Keep pressure on it," he said, nodding toward Morgan's bloodied knee. The other medic resumed their position, mumbling an apology. Seriously, though, what kind of army medic can't handle dry heaving? Shane thought.

Morgan's breath hitched, and Shane began stroking her hair. "It's ok," he whispered. "You're ok." Later, Morgan would need surgery, more than one, to repair the torn muscles. Physical rehab, too. The knee would pain her on and off for years, but mostly she would learn to live with it. In fact, she got so good at just dealing with it on her own that Shane had no idea how often it really bothered her. What he did know was that it was more often than Morgan let on.

A warm hand on his shoulder startled Shane back into the present, sitting in front of the fire and passing around a flask of rum. Morgan's hand was still on his skin. "Are you coming to bed?" It was such a normal question that he nearly forgot what they were doing in the middle of the woods. They could have been camping or making s'mores in their backyard. Adam was already gone, and Zoe and Jiao Ming were speaking to each other in hushed voices on the other side of the fire.

"Yeah, of course." Shane took Morgan's hand and followed her to their makeshift beds. She was no longer limping like before, but she still favored her right leg.

"Hey, Morgan?" Morgan looked over at him. The stars reflected in her eyes.

He didn't say anything else, but she seemed to understand. She took a step toward him and reached up to put his face in her hands. When they kissed, Shane could almost believe they were back home.

Chapter Ten

Jiao Ming, it turned out, was the best at finding edible berries and fungi. Isla often offered to go with her, feeling a bit guilty; she thought if she ate meat like the rest of them, they probably wouldn't bother foraging. When she voiced her belief to Jiao Ming, Jiao Ming dismissed it. "I kind of like foraging," she admitted. "It's quiet. Away from everything."

"What do you mean?"

"It's, well, it's just nice to think about nuts and mushrooms instead of having to start over. Again." She gave Isla an unsteady smile. They paused at a flowering bush, and Jiao Ming plucked several handfuls of purple berries. She added them to the tote bag she usually left in her backpack.

Isla frowned. What was it Jiao Ming referred to herself as? That acronym? "You mentioned you had been DACA," she said, remembering. "They just took it away?"

The muscles in Jiao Ming's face tensed. "Supreme Court reversal. Like what they did to abortion. And gay marriage."

They lapsed into silence. How had Isla not known about any of this? How had the first person to even mention the Supreme Court to her been Ms. Yo—Morgan?

Because they don't want you to know, she thought. It's easier for them that way. She wasn't entirely sure who they were, but the thought filled her with rage. It was an oddly comforting feeling.

Isla and Jiao Ming walked back into camp just as the last of the sun's rays disappeared behind the trees. Isla approached Morgan, who was cooking a fish over the fire. "I want to learn how to shoot a gun."

To Isla, it was like the world stopped. Jiao Ming stared, the bag of foraged food at her feet, threatening to spill. Adam and Shane both looked up from their conversation. Hannah and Zoe were skinning squirrels behind her, but Isla knew they were listening.

Morgan set the fish aside. "You know it's illegal for anyone without a permit to shoot a gun, right?" Everyone in Militum had one, of course. Actually, it was pretty easy to get one. Just probably not for an eighteen-year-old trans girl.

But Isla could tell it was a test. So she answered with more of Morgan's own words: "Just because something is illegal doesn't mean it's wrong."

A beat, and then Morgan's face split into a huge grin. "I'll teach you," she said. To their captive audience she asked, "Anyone else want to learn?"

Hannah put her hand up, followed by a hesitant Jiao Ming, and then Shane. Zoe laughed. "Bet this isn't the kind of teaching you had in mind when you started the school year, huh?"

"Not at all." Morgan picked up the stick supporting the fish and resumed rotating it over the fire.

* * *

The following evening, when they set up camp, Morgan also set up a series of hanging objects to use as targets. "You're not worried about wasting ammo?" Shane asked.

"We have a town stop coming up," Adam said, handing Shane his gun.

"It's weird to see you holding a gun," Morgan said, coming up behind Shane. "A little sexy though."

"Guns are not sexy," Shane protested. "They're killing machines, and I hate that this is necessary."

Hannah nudged Isla, who was holding Zoe's gun. "Must be even weirder to watch your teacher flirt with her husband," Hannah whispered. Isla giggled.

"Alright," Adam bellowed. "Morgan will show you what to do, since she's the best shot."

The image of her parents' killers lying bleeding on the ground swam to the forefront of Hannah's mind. She pushed it aside as Morgan raised her gun and shot three times in a row. She hit three of the objects: a squirrel skin from yesterday right through the eye, a can they'd picked up on the day's journey through the town center, and a leaf along the spine. Zoe rewarded her with a low whistle.

Morgan pointed her gun at the ground. "First lesson," she said, "never point your gun at anything you're not intending to shoot. That's how you kill people." Jiao Ming laughed nervously, but no one else said anything.

Morgan showed them how to hold their guns, how to check to see if it was loaded. Isla and Shane were the first to fire.

BANG! BANG! Hannah threw her hands over her ears on instinct and quickly lowered them, not wanting the group to think her weak. Still, she had to take several deep breaths to bring herself back into that moment, to clear her vision.

"Not bad," Morgan said. Isla had managed to hit one of the larger targets: a dead fish. Hannah knew she was actually aiming for the crumpled piece of paper about half a foot to the left, but Morgan didn't need to know that. Besides, Shane hadn't managed to hit anything.

Isla gave the gun to Hannah, and Hannah took a shooting stance. Like Shane, Hannah managed to miss the targets altogether, but forgetting that, she actually felt fierce holding Zoe's gun, like a fighter, like someone who'd been doing this for years. Like she could actually do this.

* * *

As though they were telepathically linked, Morgan almost always woke up when Shane did. Their time evading the law in the middle of the woods did nothing to change that. She could still sense him waking up from a separate hammock. When she opened her bleary eyes, it was nearly four o'clock in the morning according to her watch, and Shane was stumbling away from the campsite.

Morgan frowned. She got up quickly and quietly followed him, rounding the corner just in time to watch him vomit into a bush. He gagged and heaved again, but nothing came up. Morgan placed her hand on the small of his back and felt Shane sigh. "I'm ok," he gasped. "Too little dinner, too much to drink." Zoe had broken out the rum again, this time with Isla and Hannah present, although she didn't offer them any.

"Hmm." Morgan rubbed his back as he leaned forward and retched again. He was shivering now in the heat of the night.

Finally, he spat the taste out of his mouth and sank to his

knees. Morgan went down with him, sitting to his left and turning to face him. "You didn't drink that much." She took his hand. "Do you want to talk about it?"

Shane took a deep breath. "I was just dreaming. About . . ." He trailed off, but Morgan understood. "Yeah. It was pretty gross."

"Gross isn't the right word for it," he said. "I thought I would lose you before I even got to know you." His voice broke, and his eyes sparkled with suppressed tears.

"Babe, they shot me in the knee, not the head." She lifted her hand to his face and stroked his cheek. He leaned into her touch, letting his tears fall onto her fingertips.

"I just can never forget how much pain you were in," he said. "I can't stand that it still hurts you."

"I'm ok," she said. "Really." Truly, the pain subsided immensely after their day of not moving. And if it still ached a bit, that was something Shane didn't need to know. Not yet, anyway.

For a moment, Morgan's mind took her back to the time when she was pregnant. The news had been unexpected and unwanted. She hated the whole experience—her body expanding out of her control, and the parasite in her womb taking her over. After, she exercised like a fiend, trying to rid her body of the experience, until Shane begged her to stop before she hurt herself.

She and Shane had been together for several years when she learned she was carrying his biological child. She told him she didn't want it, didn't want anything that would remind her of familiar faces hovering over hers and thunder roaring, drowning out her own throat-searing screams. She didn't want to remember the pain between her legs and then the pain nestled in her heart.

She had been terrified of Shane's reaction, but he surprised her. He said that it was her choice. He spent days trying to find someone who would do an abortion that didn't involve a back alley and a hanger. And when he couldn't find one, he handled the adoption because he said Morgan shouldn't have to. He was always brave in those quiet, unglamorous ways. He was always brave for her.

Shane cleared his throat and sat up straighter. "I don't know what I'd do without you," he said.

Morgan offered him a half smile. "Well, good thing you're stuck with me. We left our marriage certificate behind." She stood. "Good luck trying to return me without the receipt." She put out her hand for him to take, and he did, now matching her half-hearted grin with his own.

Chapter Eleven

Thunder jolted Zoe out of a deep sleep. All around her, the others sat up, alerted to the rapidly changing weather by the roaring of the sky. Immediately, Zoe could tell this wasn't going to be a storm they should just ride out. Beside her, Adam tumbled out of his hammock and yelled, "Get your stuff and follow me! There's a safe house not far from here."

"That would've been nice to know," Zoe mumbled as she threw her backpack over her shoulders. It began to downpour just as they started walking, and Zoe, who had resumed her position in the back, covered her head with her arms. She could barely see Isla and Hannah, not a foot in front of her.

After nearly an hour of stumbling through the downpour, they arrived at a small house with red shutters on the outskirts of the woods. Adam knocked, and a tall woman with curly, brown hair and a jagged scar through her eyebrow opened the door. "Boeck?"

"Hey Mayaan." He smiled weakly and the woman, Mayaan, ushered them all inside.

"I'll set up rooms," she said once they were all safely in her kitchen. "And I think I have clothes that'll fit most of you."

"Thank you," Adam said. Mayaan raced up the stairs, and he checked in with the rest of the group. "Everyone ok?"

They all nodded except Morgan, who mumbled something about finding a bathroom. She darted off, shivering a bit. Zoe followed Morgan with her eyes. It was raining, sure, and they were all drenched to the bone, but it certainly wasn't cold enough to shiver. In fact, the night was uncomfortably humid.

Adam slipped into Mayaan's room after all the others were shown theirs. "You forgot to give me a bed," he teased.

Mayaan started toward him, smirking. "What a shame," she said. "We'll have to share." She grabbed at the front of his shirt and kissed him, hard.

"Adam? Are you in there?"

He sighed and pressed his forehead against Mayaan's. "It's Zoe," he said.

"You should see what she needs." We can continue this later," she said, gesturing between the two of them. She opened the door, and Zoe marched in.

"We need to talk."

Mayaan slid out of the room, gently pulling the door shut behind her. Adam sat on the bed. "What's up?"

"Why didn't I know about this place?" she asked.

Adam blinked. "What?"

"I had no idea this woman was here. We're supposed to be leading this mission together," she said. "Or am I just a refugee?"

"You're not just a refugee, Zo, but you're not leading this mission."

"Fine." She threw up her hands. "Fine, then. I get it." She went to storm out when Adam stood and said, "Wait."

"Wait for what?" Zoe did leave then, slamming the door

behind her. Adam sat back at the edge of the bed, scowling. Who was Zoe to judge him? She had no idea what he'd been through.

Somehow, the thought only made him feel worse.

*　*　*

Shane wrapped his arms around Morgan in their temporary bed. It was rather short, and Shane had to keep his knees a bit bent, but he didn't really mind. It was a real bed, after all.

Thunder cracked overhead like a whip, and Morgan cried out. "Shh," Shane whispered. "It's ok. You're here. It's just me and you, ok? You're safe here. Nothing is going to happen to you." He brushed her hair back from her forehead and placed a gentle kiss there, a reminder. She shuddered and gripped his wrist.

"Don't let go."

"I won't. I won't let go."

She turned so that her hair covered her face again, her head pressed against his chest. Still, Shane could tell she was crying by the way her body trembled. "Talk to me," she murmured. "Please."

Shane felt his own eyes water. He wished he could take away her pain. Instead, he said, "Ok. Uh. Did I ever tell you about the time my sister and I went searching for turtles?" They both knew he had, but Morgan shook her head, and Shane said, "We were visiting my grandparents, and they had a stream pretty close to their place, so we got it into our heads that we could get a pair of turtles and keep them in a jar, since we didn't have a tank." He began toying with Morgan's hair as he spoke, running his fingers through it and separating it into soft strands. Anything to bring her back to now. "I must have been seven or eight. We went down to the stream together and changed our minds the moment one of the turtles snapped at us." He hadn't seen his sister in a while. He might never be able to again.

"Mom and Dad were so mad that we'd snuck off," he continued, "especially at Ja'Nesha, since she's older. But when we told them why we went, they promised to get us a turtle. It was a nice gesture, but we both screamed in terror and ran the other way."

He looked down at Morgan, no longer shaking. He brushed her hair from her face one more time and found her eyes closed; the adrenaline of the night had finally run its course. Shane pressed a gentle kiss on her forehead and closed his own eyes, never letting go as he slid into his own dreams.

* * *

The storm lasted another three days. On their first full day there, when the storm finally calmed from thunder and lightning to roof-rattling winds and raindrops the size of bullets, Mayaan brought a few board games up from the basement. "I know it's not helpful," she said, "but maybe it'll take your mind off things."

Shane picked a deck of cards off the top. "Thank you," he murmured.

Across the room, Hannah eyed the stack. She loved games, especially Sails, her mom's favorite, and Power Trip, which were both in the pile. Hannah knew, too, that she could use a distraction, particularly from the anxiety building in the pit of her stomach, creating nauseating cramps. But she also remained painfully aware of how much younger she was than most of their crew, and thus refrained from getting outwardly excited in case it reminded the rest of the room that she was still technically a child. Instead, she waited for Shane to ask her if she wanted in before wandering over. "What are you playing?"

Shane looked over at Jiao Ming. "Savage?" She and Hannah nodded—Hannah vaguely remembered playing the game with her grandparents years ago—and Shane dealt the cards.

*　*　*

"Whachya got there?"

Isla whirled around, ready to throw the book in her hand, but it was just Zoe, her own hands above her head. "Whoa, sorry. Door was open."

"Sorry. Just thought you might be—"

"An officer. Believe me, I get it." Zoe sat on the edge of the queen-sized bed Isla and Hannah were sharing. "Good book?"

"Adam let me borrow it from his place," Isla told her. "It's Howard Zinn."

"Who?" Zoe took the book and studied the cover.

"I heard Ms. Young, Morgan, mention the name in class once. He's a historian."

"If Morgan likes him, he must be banned." She handed the book back to Isla. "Can I borrow it when you're done?"

"Yeah. Of course."

The door opened again, and Hannah walked in, stopping when she saw Zoe in the room. "Oh, I was looking for you."

"Me?" Zoe gestured toward herself, and Hannah said, "Yeah. Can we talk for a second?"

"Should I leave?" Isla asked.

"No." Hannah shut the door behind her. Deep breath. "I got my period."

"Oh?" Zoe raised an eyebrow. "Ok?"

"For . . . for the first time."

"But . . . really?"

Hannah hesitated. "I know, it's really late. But I just didn't, I mean I don't know—"

"You don't know what to do."

"Could you, um, help me? I guess this is the kind of thing I should ask my mom about, but . . ." she trailed off, biting her lip.

"Yeah," Zoe said. "I can help you." She put a hand on Hannah's back and maneuvered her to the bathroom off the bedroom. "Let me get you a tampon, ok?"

"Thank you. I really—"

"Don't worry about it. Actually, I didn't get my period until I was like fifteen."

"Really?" Hannah seemed to brighten at that, and Zoe couldn't help but smile. It was actually one of Zoe's sisters who had gotten her period late, but Hannah didn't need to know that.

"Really. I'll be right back." Zoe left, and Hannah glanced awkwardly at Isla. "Sorry."

"Why are you sorry?" Isla asked. "You're right. You should be home right now with Mom. And she should be teaching you how to do this, not Zoe."

"Complaining isn't going to change it, though."

"But you're allowed to be sad." Isla took a breath. "You're only here because you came to rescue me—"

"Don't do that," Hannah interrupted, suddenly furious. "I'd do it a hundred times for you. A thousand. I'd do anything for you."

"I know that," Isla said. "But anything should be, like, not telling Dad when I have sex for the first time or covering for me when I don't want to do to some family event. Not breaking me out of jail. This really is fucked up."

"Yeah."

Isla took a breath. "We never really talked about Mom and Dad."

Hannah frowned. "We did. That night we were at Adam's."

"But not since. I miss them." She did, especially in moments like now. Moments when they were safest, when her mind could focus not on survival, but on what she had lost. It was painful to remember. But she wanted to. She owed it to her parents and to Hannah.

A pause. "I miss them, too." Hannah's voice broke on the last word, and she squeezed her hands into fists. "I keep seeing them die in my dreams." A single tear escaped, then another. "I don't know what we'll do."

Isla went over to her sister and pulled her into a tight hug. She wished she could be stronger for Hannah. But she knew Hannah was trying to be strong for her, too. "Whatever it is, we'll do it together. Ok? I'll never leave you."

Hannah nodded. "I know." But neither of them did, really. What if something happened to one of them while they were escaping?

Zoe came back in, and Hannah wiped at her eyes. "You ready?" Zoe asked. Hannah nodded, and Zoe followed her into the bathroom.

<u>Chapter Twelve</u>

The thunder picked up again as the group, minus Hannah, sat down to dinner. "She wasn't feeling well," Zoe said, locking eyes with Isla. "We can save something for her."

"Yeah, that's fine," Mayaan said, serving herself a spoonful of mashed potatoes. "The beds are ok and everything? I know some of them are a bit small."

"They're great," Isla said. "Thank you so much." Thunder boomed again, nearly in sync with the lightning outside.

Across the table, Morgan stood. "You ok?" Shane asked.

Morgan glanced around, seemed to realize everyone was watching her. "I . . . yeah, I'll come back down later. Just tired." She forced a small smile for Shane and placed a gentle hand on his shoulder. "You stay." He did, but he still watched her leave, worry evident on his face.

"Do we have any idea when this rain is supposed to stop?" Zoe asked between bites. All of them, near-starving after living so long on fish, berries, fungi, and the occasional squirrel, or in Isla's case, just berries and fungi, were forcing themselves to slow down.

"Not for a while," Mayaan told her.

Zoe clenched her fist tighter around her fork. Their only

hope now was that the rest of the groups they were supposed to meet up with were also held up by the rain.

*   *   *

Morgan sat against the pale aspen headboard on the bed she shared with Shane, her knees to her chest under a periwinkle blanket. He had come by briefly, but Morgan insisted she just needed some time alone. Now, she regretted sending him away. His presence would have been a welcome distraction from her shallow breathing and rising nausea. *In. Out. In. Out.*

The light rapping on the door let her know whoever it was, it wasn't Shane, and she had no real desire to see anyone else. Still, she called, "Come in."

Zoe cracked the door open. "Hey. I just . . . you seemed a little on edge the past day or so. I just wanted to make sure you were ok."

"Oh. Thanks."

Zoe took a tentative step forward to where Morgan sat. She held a mug out. "I brought you tea. You, uh, said you liked it at one point, I think. I don't remember when."

Actually, Morgan never would have said that, the sheer amount of willpower it took to overcome her dependence on caffeine, but she didn't have to mention that to Zoe. Morgan opened her mouth to reply when thunder cracked like a whip outside her window. She jumped and pulled the blanket up to her shoulders. Once the echoes died down, she managed a shaky laugh for Zoe's sake. "I guess I'm a little on edge, yes." She reached out for the mug. Zoe passed it over.

"Sure. Well, if you ever need to, you know, talk, I'm around." Zoe hesitated, then turned for the door.

"I was raped during a thunder storm," Morgan said. Zoe froze, but she was clearly listening, so Morgan continued, staring at a dark spot on the wall. She wasn't sure what possessed her to say anything, but she continued, "They were men in my unit. They waited for a big storm to cover up my screams. The thunder and the wind and the rain." Morgan gripped her mug tighter, the porcelain biting into her skin a distraction from the words coming out of her mouth. "Big storms like this, they bring me back to that. Not that I'm seeing it in my head or anything, but I'm just, just frozen and . . . my body feels it. I guess that doesn't make sense."

"No, it does." Zoe came around to the other side of the bed and sat beside Morgan. "Um. When I was sixteen, I was dating this girl, Aviva." Zoe's whole face lit up when she said the name. "I guess someone reported us because they took her away. The person who reported us didn't know who I was, though, and I guess Aviva never ratted me out." Zoe hugged her knees to her chest, mimicking Morgan, and continued, "Sometimes when something reminds me of that, like, a comment or whatever, I feel so cold all over. And just . . . so angry."

"I'm sorry."

"It was a long time ago." Zoe unwrapped her legs and turned to face Morgan. "Does Shane know? You know . . . ."

"He does. We weren't together at the time. We met in the army and became friends, and after the war ended, he came and found me . . . ."

Zoe waited, but Morgan didn't continue. For weeks after the rape, Morgan wondered why those men would hurt her like that when they were supposed to be on her side. She came to realize that those men weren't good people just because they were on what she considered the right side. They thought they were going to win the war. That was why they fought; there was no moral or ethical basis to their service. It's easier to fight for something when you think you're on the winning side. Those men were simply opportunists, and, she realized with a twinge in her gut, she was just another opportunity.

But perhaps she knew that all along. Perhaps it was easier to maintain denial.

As though she was reading Morgan's thoughts, Zoe said, "I guess we are kind of fighting a losing battle, huh?"

"No. I can't believe that. Not after everything." She looked at Zoe with wild, desperate eyes. "There has to be a chance." Thunder roared overhead, and Morgan jumped, sending her tea sloshing around the inside of her mug.

"Hey." Zoe took the mug and set it aside so that she could take Morgan's trembling hand in hers. "You're safe. You're safe here."

Slowly, Morgan brought herself back to the moment. She was there, in a stranger's room, with Zoe in the middle of a thunder storm. She felt the fabric of the blanket on the pads of her fingers, the lumpy mattress beneath her legs. For now, she was safe. They were all safe.

"Ok," she said. "I'm ok." She pulled away from Zoe, suddenly shy. "Really, you don't have to stay."

"I don't mind. Besides," she joked. "I have nowhere else to be." She pulled Morgan close to her again, and Morgan let herself rest her head on Zoe's shoulder.

*　　*　　*

Zoe waited for Morgan to fall asleep before sneaking back

downstairs. Jiao Ming and Shane were the only ones left, sitting on the couch by the fireplace. "Where is everyone?"

"Asleep," Jiao Ming said. "Where were you?"

"Talking to Morgan." To Shane, she said, "She's sleeping now."

Shane yawned and stretched. "Time for me to turn in, too." He stood and yawned again. "G'night."

"Night, Shane," Jiao Ming said at the same time Zoe said, "Night." He was halfway up the stairs when Jiao Ming asked Zoe, "Ready for bed, too?"

"Yeah." Zoe waited for Shane's footsteps to fade before adding, "Actually, there's something I want to say." Jiao Ming frowned, and Zoe launched into her story. She told Jiao Ming about Aviva, how they were young and in love, and how a neighbor saw them kiss one day and reported it to the local police. She explained how she never saw Aviva again, how she waited every day for months to be taken away, too.

"She's a lot of the reason I do what I do. You know, with the revolution." Zoe hid her shaking hands under her legs and waited for a response. Jiao Ming opened her mouth, but Zoe blurted, "I understand if this is too much."

"No, Zoe stop it." Jiao Ming shifted so that she could face Zoe. "I don't know what to say to that. I mean, thank you for telling me. That's awful, Zo."

"I guess I just wanted you to know. Since, well, I love you." Zoe shut her eyes then so she didn't have to watch Jiao Ming's reaction. She knew it was true, and she wanted to say it. But she also knew she couldn't bear it if Jiao Ming looked too shocked or scared or, God forbid, amused.

"Zoe?" Zoe opened her eyes again and saw Jiao Ming grinning ear to ear. "I love you, too."

Zoe flushed. "Well. Good then."

Jiao Ming laughed. "C'mon," she said. "Let's go to bed."

"Like, bed-bed? Or . . ."

"Let's get some rest," Jiao Ming said. "Then tomorrow we'll be plenty ready to do the or."

"I'll look forward to it," Zoe teased. They went upstairs together and found their room. Both of them stumbled into bed, the adrenaline of the day fading, and fell asleep almost immediately.

They finally left Mayaan's place at far too early an hour several days behind schedule. "I told you we shouldn't have taken that day," Zoe grumbled. She and Adam hadn't spoken since she'd confronted him in Mayaan's room.

"Please give it a rest," Adam sighed. "I get it. It was a bad idea."

"We should get to the other refugees by tomorrow, though, right?" Hannah asked as they started walking.

"Day after at most," Adam replied. More to himself he said, "It won't be long now."

That evening, to commemorate their last night together, Zoe broke out the rum. "You want to try?" she asked, passing it to Isla.

Their group had set up their final campsite deep in the woods, just past a faded, faceup Welcome to Colorado sign. Zoe and Hannah made a fireplace while Morgan and Jiao Ming hunted and foraged, respectfully. Now, they were food-sleepy around the fire and enjoying each other's company.

"They're still kids," Morgan protested, but Hannah cut her off. "I'll try some," she said.

Zoe made to pass it over to Hannah, who was sitting to

her left, but Isla snatched it back and took a swig. Shane, Jiao Ming, and Zoe laughed. Morgan frowned.

"You know, Morgan, you're not her teacher anymore," Shane said, but Morgan just sighed.

"They're still underage," she murmured as Zoe passed the rum to Hannah, who took a sip and immediately choked. Jiao Ming understood where Morgan was coming from: As much as Isla and Hannah had already seen, she thought they should get to keep some of their innocence. It was what her parents had tried to do for her even after they were deported. But it hadn't worked.

"Hey, where's Adam?" Shane asked. Jiao Ming frowned. "Not sure. I'll go look for him."

Jiao Ming stood and Zoe turned suddenly serious. "On your own?"

"I'll be fine." Jiao Ming wandered off in the direction of the path, hoping Adam hadn't gone too far. She found him sitting on a rock on the side of the path, pressing his hands against his forehead. "You ok?"

Adam jumped. "Y-yeah. What are you doing here?"

"Looking for you," Jiao Ming said, squatting next to him. "Headache?"

He gave her a small smile. "Just tired," he said. "I . . . I'm ready for this to be over."

"Me too." She bit her lip in hesitation before she said, "Thank you, by the way. I was . . . well, I don't know what would have happened to me if you hadn't helped me. So. Thanks."

Adam's heart skipped a beat. "Don't thank me yet," he said.

Jiao Ming returned his smile. "Whatever happens from

here, you tried." She put a hand on his shoulder. "Sleep. We'll try to keep it down." She squeezed, then she got up, walked back to the campsite, and settled between Isla and Shane.

"We're talking about what we're looking forward to in California," Shane told her. "Morgan said connecting with organizers—"

"Of course she did."

"And Hannah said sleeping in a real bed."

"And chocolate," Hannah added with a giggle.

Jiao Ming shot her a smile. "Makes sense. I'm looking forward to chocolate, too."

Zoe scooted forward, closer to the fire. "I'm ready not to have to hide," she said. "Not hiding my work, and not having to worry about getting arrested for kissing a girl." She said this last part with a pointed glance at Jiao Ming, who blushed.

"I like that," Isla said. "I know California isn't going to be a magical country of acceptance or whatever, but it would be really nice not to have to worry about any of that." None of them were entirely sure what the country would be like. For all they'd done, none of them had ever actually been there. She wasn't sure why, but Jiao Ming pictured hills and green grass. Which she knew was stupid because the whole country wouldn't look the same.

"Anyway, I'd like that," Isla said. "Just to have people be more open."

"I can't even imagine," Morgan said.

"It would be really cool to meet people who are also, you know, out," Isla added. "I didn't even know what being trans was until I was thirteen. I thought there was something wrong with me." She bit her lip and fell silent.

"It's lonely," Zoe said. "It's obviously not the same, but I felt really alone, too."

"I think the part that's most exciting to me is finally having a home," Jiao Ming said. "Even if I'm not a citizen in California, they won't have that same threat of deporting me to hang over my head. It's a good feeling." She hesitated and added, "That, and the whole making out with girls thing." She winked at Zoe, who blew her a kiss.

"I agree with Hannah about the bed," Shane said. "Just the whole idea of being safe. Not worrying that Morgan's work will get her arrested or killed."

"Cute," Zoe said. "Morgan, no kissing girls for you?"

"I'm very happily married."

"Tragic," Zoe sighed, taking a drink. "You would have made a great closeted bisexual."

"Who's closeted? I'm just also monogamous." Zoe nearly choked, and Shane laughed.

"Alright, we should get to bed," Morgan said with a smirk. "It's getting late." They all got up, and Jiao Ming kicked dirt over the fire to put it out. Mostly, she'd already forgotten about Adam and the interaction that might have seemed odd if she wasn't already so grateful to the man.

Chapter Thirteen

The seven of them arrived in a clearing around midday. Morgan saw Isla freeze at the sight of so many people she didn't know after so many weeks of just their makeshift family, and she put a hand on Isla's shoulder. Part of Morgan wondered if they would all stay together. Whatever Adam, Jiao Ming, and Zoe did, she would watch over the girls.

As a child, Morgan had cousins that lived in Colorado Springs, a mere two or three hours from where she sat now. Or, what used to be Colorado Springs. It had seemed so odd when the borders first began to change after California left, when the former state took land that had previously belonged to the U.S. It was part of the deal, no doubt: California was able to secede because the new government knew California and its many citizens posed less of a threat to the regime as a separate country rather than a state with a vote.

Morgan was irate when she heard this. How could they leave just like that? The thought still made her angry. Now though, California had been its own country for more than half her life and for all of Isla's and Hannah's. There was no more Colorado Springs or even Colorado. She wondered what the country would look like if they ever did manage to overthrow Powers.

A teen around Isla's age with curly, blue hair and a T-shirt that read "SURF'S UP" approached them. "Hey, I'm Taylor," they said. "I'm one of the volunteers from Border Brothers."

"I'm Adam. We're the group from Evanston."

"Cool. We all got a little held up by the rain, it looks like. We're just waiting on two more groups, and then we can move." Taylor gestured toward the picnic blanket behind them. Or, more accurately, to the food on it. "Help yourself in the meantime."

They grabbed what food they could and wandered off to a quiet space away from the other groups. Zoe bit into a chicken leg and actually moaned.

"Calm down," Jiao Ming said, but she was laughing.

"Dude, try this." She handed Jiao Ming the leg and grabbed a peach instead.

Another group wandered into their camp, and Taylor immediately greeted them. "I really like to imagine the look on the officer's faces after a successful mission," Morgan admitted to the rest of them.

"Ugh. Officer Bryant," Zoe grumbled. "He was the one I thought would get me in the end, for sure."

"Sergeant Shore," Adam added, his mind on the last group, ten minutes away. The group that would actually be a raiding party. "Smug little fuck."

"Sergeant?" Morgan asked.

"Christian Shore."

"How do you know him?"

Adam's heart nearly stopped. "What?"

"How do you know Christian Shore?" Morgan repeated. "He was the officer that interrogated me back in Evanston."

He hesitated. "Maybe you mentioned him to me."

Morgan's eyes narrowed. "I doubt it." She hadn't talked about her interrogation with anyone.

"Maybe, uh, Shane. Or Isla. Or maybe I ran into him at one point, you know—"

"You called him Sergeant," Hannah said, coming to stand by Morgan. "Shore was an officer when Isla knew him."

Adam glared in Hannah's direction, and Morgan put the pieces together. Shore must have been promoted since Isla escaped.

Which meant Adam was in contact with the Militum.

"Adam?" He couldn't look at her, couldn't look at her face. She felt a decisive, white-hot hatred building in her stomach. After everything they had been through.

"What's going on?" Shane asked, standing too.

"Fucker's dirty," Zoe said, her hands trembling with fury. "Is there even another party coming?" Slowly, Adam shook his head.

"Shit, shit, shit. We have to get out of here." She sprinted back to the main group, and Adam finally gathered the courage to look at Morgan and immediately recoiled at her expression. *Good.*

"Can I have everyone's attention?" Zoe was now standing on a stump, her hands cupped around her mouth to amplify her voice. The chatter died down, and she said, "Our mission has been compromised, and there are officers close by." Immediately, a soft murmur began among the others, but she kept going. "We need to get to the border as quickly as possible. Guides and volunteers, lead the way."

Almost as soon as Zoe stepped off her stump, the steady murmurs of worry became full-blown panic. The remaining guides gathered their groups fairly quickly, and soon people were running out of the clearing in frantic clumps.

Morgan stood over Adam still. He owed her answers. "What about Mayaan?" she asked. "And Arnie?"

Adam, once again, averted his gaze. "Dead," he mumbled. "Both dead. Jackson Shore told me they were or would be."

She didn't know who Jackson was, but that didn't matter. "You're a real piece of shit," she hissed. Her fingers momentarily twitched toward her gun. Adam closed his eyes in anticipation, but Shane grabbed her hand before she could make a move. She took a breath and left Adam sitting there, alone. She had bigger worries right now than the snake she formerly considered a friend.

The pain built in Morgan's knee as they ran, until she couldn't take it anymore. She stumbled over a tree root, and agony radiated down her leg. "Shane, stop." Shane whipped around. Morgan was listing heavily to the right. Her left hand, the hand not in Shane's, was holding her knee. "I can't keep up," she gasped, leaning heavily against a pine tree. The others were already far ahead of them. There was no one else around.

"You'll ride on my back." He turned back, so she could do so. "C'mon."

"No. They'll catch us."

"They won't."

"They will," Morgan said, putting her hand on Shane's cheek. She knew what she had to do. "Please. Take care of the girls for me."

Tears sprang into Shane's eyes. "No. No. You can't go back alone."

"Do it for me." Morgan was crying now, too, but she kept speaking. "Please. Do everything you can to take these fuckers down. I'll hold them off for as long as I can."

"I can't."

"You can," Morgan said fiercely. "You have to. I'll find you. I'll—"

Shane kissed her, hard and slow. They stood together, swaying, for forever, or for never enough. They broke apart, and he slowly backed away. "Be careful," he whispered. Morgan bit her lip and limped as quickly as she could back the way they came. She felt Shane watching her as she vanished through the trees. She only hoped that he would have the strength to run.

*　　*　　*

Adam was still sitting in the clearing when Jackson Shore and his men appeared. He looked up at the captain and said, "They figured it out."

Jackson Shore's face remained impassive but for the small twitch of his eyebrow. He turned back to his men. "Find them."

Just like that, fifty men bolted into the forest, leaving Adam alone with Jackson Shore, his son the sergeant, and another ten or so officers.

Night fell before any of them moved. Two men appeared from between the trees, supporting a third figure between them. Adam nearly yelled when he saw her fall to her knees, a shadow of pain over her bruised face. How did they capture Morgan?

The elder Shore approached. "Was she all you could find?"

Somewhat defensively, the officer on Morgan's left said, "She had a gun. She killed twelve men."

Christian stepped forward. "She's the one who escaped

Evanston Prison, Sir."

Jackson squatted in front of Morgan so that they were face to face. "You killed twelve of my men, did you?"

"It's a shame," Morgan spat, glaring. "I meant to kill more."

Jackson frowned. Adam tried to regulate his breathing. They couldn't kill her, right? They needed her. She had information.

Christian moved to stand by his father's side. "Where are the others?"

Morgan glared at the younger Shore. "In California by now."

"Why'd they leave you behind?" Christian asked.

Morgan smiled sweetly. "I'm the best shot," she said. A thin trickle of blood leaked from the corner of her mouth.

Jackson's eyes narrowed. "Take her," he said.

One of the men beside Morgan hauled her up by her shoulder. Another held a gun to her head. Hands raised, Morgan let them lead her to a van. Adam watched three of the officers get in with her as two of the others moved to sit up front. They would wait a while in the hope that they could capture some of the other revolutionaries, he knew. And then they would take her back to Virginia, if she was lucky.

They didn't shut the truck doors. At least, not while Adam was sitting there. He watched one of the men stand suddenly and saw Morgan stare up at him like she wasn't helpless. Until he slapped her so hard across the face that Adam felt her pain as his own.

* * *

Isla grabbed Hannah's hand just as Jiao Ming took hers. They ran through the trees as fast as they could, Isla keeping her gaze on Taylor's blue hair just ahead of them. They had to make it.

She didn't see Zoe, Shane, or Morgan. She would just have to trust that they were behind them, somewhere. And then out of nowhere, Zoe came up behind them and grabbed Hannah's hand. "Go!" she yelled, and they sped up. Isla kept her eyes on that blue head of hair. As long as she had Taylor in her sights, they would make it. As long as they were following Taylor, they would be ok.

It was maybe irrational. But she had to have something.

Chest heaving, legs burning, the four of them sprinted after the group. After half an hour at least, they burst into a clearing, the border just visible on the other side. Along the fence separating the two countries were guard posts, with three people that Isla could see in each. Zoe and Jiao Ming both sped up, and Isla strained to match their pace.

A sudden, terrifying thought: Would they be allowed in?

Much of what happened next was a blur for Isla. They were at the fence, then beyond it. The four of them collapsed just outside a large building with white trim, Taylor and some of the other volunteers waiting outside. Somewhere in the distance, she heard someone shouting, and then she had water in her hand. She untwisted the cap and poured it on her face.

After the moment it took to clear her head, she turned to Hannah, panting next to her. "We made it," she gasped. She reached out and grasped Hannah's hand. Both of them were crying. They made it.

And nothing would ever be the same again.

*   *   *

Jiao Ming was the first to spot Shane when he came through the door, the sun setting behind him. She ran to him and put a hand on his arm. "Are you ok? What took you so long? Where's Morgan?"

Shane sank to the floor. "She's not coming," he said. Then he buried his face in his hands and burst into tears.

Zoe joined them, her heart tight. She crouched next to Shane. "What happened?"

Between sobs, Shane said, "She c-couldn't keep up b-because of her knee. She went back to h-hold them off . . ." he trailed off, shaking too hard to speak. Zoe wrapped her arms around him and pressed her cheek to his. Bile rose in Zoe's throat at the thought of Morgan at the mercy of the Militum, unable to escape.

Just like Aviva.

Behind them, Zoe heard Isla sob and Hannah murmur something too quiet for her to make out. The others in the hall eyed them sadly, realizing someone had been left behind. Zoe ignored them. Soon, she couldn't tell which wet spots on her cheeks were Shane's tears and which were her own.

She held him until he pulled away, still gasping. "I t-tried to get her to come. She was in too m-much p-pain."

"I know." Zoe took his hand and held fast. "She'll find us again. She will."

"Wh-what if she can't?"

"We can't think that way," Jiao Ming said, wiping the tears from Shane's face. They were all crying at this point. "She has to." She glanced at Zoe, who nodded, and Jiao Ming repeated, "She just has to."

Chapter Fourteen

One moment, her own screams sounded faint to her, like she was watching the birth from a distance and with headphones on. The next, she thought she might split her own ear drums. The pain racked her body and threatened to turn her inside out. On her left, Shane squeezed her hand, telling her to breathe. At her feet, a midwife encouraged her to push, push harder, just pushhaaaahhhhhhhhh!

And then it was done. At the end of the bed, the midwife cut the cord, and a small, filthy creature screamed in a nurse's arms. The nurse looked uncertainly at Shane and Morgan. "Do you want to hold him?"

Shane shook his head, and then they were gone. It was just the two of them, like always. Morgan began to cry then, harder than she ever had. She had made the right choice, and she wouldn't change it. That didn't make it hurt any less.

Morgan's throbbing shoulder woke her from her uneasy dream, sending fresh waves of pain through her in time with her beating heart. Right. The Militum. They'd taken her, beaten her in the van until she lost consciousness. She used her other arm to sit up and took in her surroundings with one eye, the other was swollen shut.

This cell was somehow even more dismal than the last one

she'd found herself in. Clearly, no one bothered to dust before dumping her onto the floor. The bars were covered in some sort of rust or slime, it was brownish, at any rate, and the only light came from a small, flickering fixture overhead. There was no furniture in this cell. Just a blue, peeling bucket in the corner.

Gently, Morgan prodded at her shoulder and immediately pulled back. Dislocated for sure. Taking a deep breath, she pushed it back into place.

"Fuck!" Tears sprang into her eyes, and she bit her lip, hard. She sat back against the brick wall, trying to remember how to breathe properly. She heard footsteps overhead.

Morgan nearly laughed out loud when a familiar man stepped in front of her cell. "Hey there, Officer Shore."

Christian's eyes narrowed. "It's Sergeant Shore now," he said, gesturing to his updated uniform.

"What do you want?" Her voice was thick with pain and exhaustion, but he still flinched back. The bruises on her face should make him feel better, shouldn't they? But they hurt like they were his own.

He hesitated before speaking again. "I just, I heard you yell."

Morgan did laugh now. "So what? You came to make sure I'm ok? Go fuck yourself."

"Watch it."

"Or what?" She glared up at him, and Christian couldn't quite meet her eyes, green, like his, and sharp. "What can you do to me that you haven't already done?"

Christian frowned. "You have no idea."

Morgan stood and came to the bars, sending Christian

back another step. "No, you have no idea," she spat. "You don't know what it's like to care about something more than you care about yourself. I'm willing to die for this war."

"Good! Because you might!"

She had nothing else to lose. Either they would kill her outright, or they would try to force her to give them information before killing her. "Are you evil or just stupid? Have you not noticed that most of the people you lock up look like you, Sergeant? They'll come for you too, eventually."

Christian opened his mouth to respond, and turned away instead. He left, slamming the stone door behind him and locking it in place.

*　*　*

Christian entered his father's office and frowned. "Sir?"

Jackson was pulling a short stack of papers out of the fireplace, still flaming. He stamped out the rest of the embers with his foot and looked back at Christian. "None of your concern."

"Ah. Ok." Christian cleared his throat, trying to put any follow-up questions out of his mind. "You wanted to see me, Sir?"

"I did," Jackson said. "I wanted to tell you that you did a good job on this mission."

He didn't, though. "They got away."

"Not all of them," Jackson said. "And we'll find the others. You did everything right. I'm proud of you."

Christian's lips twitched upward slightly. "Thank you, Sir."

"That will be all, Sergeant." Christian turned on his heel and left, shutting the door behind him. In the glowing warmth of his father's praise, Christian almost forgot about the burning files. Almost.

* * *

Zoe was the second of their group, now just five, to be processed. She joined Shane on the courthouse steps and put a hand on his shoulder. "Morgan will be ok." She really did believe it. Mostly.

Shane's mouth tightened into a line, but he didn't say anything. So Zoe said, "She will. I know it doesn't mean as much now, but . . . Adam used to talk about her all the time." Shane pulled a face, but Zoe kept going. "How great she was. How much she did for the revolution." She paused for a moment, picking at the edges of her nails. "I was really jealous, honestly. I had just started and wanted to be the best, like I always did. But once we started traveling together, I saw what he meant. She just . . . she knew her shit. Levelheaded. And so smart. I really couldn't help admire her. I really think if anyone can get back to us, it's her."

"Thanks, Zoe." He smiled at her, but it didn't quite reach his eyes.

Isla sat down on Shane's other side. Her eyes were just bloodshot enough that Zoe knew she had been crying. "No problems?" Zoe asked.

"No," Isla said. "You guys?" Her voice was a bit nasal too, but Zoe didn't say anything.

"No. Just waiting."

The three of them lapsed into comfortable silence, and Zoe let herself take in her new surroundings. Not that much looked very different on this side of the border. The trees were the same here, mostly spruce and pine, as were the birds. The sky was the same pale blue with a puffy cloud or two. The bus stop that would take them to their temporary home was like any ordinary American bus stop.

The license plates were different. Pale blue with black lettering. The road signs, too, which gave directions in both English and Spanish. The mountains were closer from here. There were no officers in sight, Militum or otherwise. Zoe felt different here, too. Less afraid. She hadn't recognized the weight on her chest as fear—or even much acknowledged it at all—until it lifted.

"Do you know who to get in touch with here?" Isla asked.

"What do you mean?" Zoe asked.

"Like, who in California we can talk to about helping the revolution."

"Oh. I mean, yeah. Sure."

Isla's face broke into a smile, a real one. "Great."

Zoe grinned back at her, and then turned to Shane. "You don't have to—"

"I'm in," he said.

"In what?" Jiao Ming and Hannah came up behind them on the steps.

"We can talk and walk," Zoe said. She stood up and reached for Jiao Ming's hand. Together, the five of them walked over to the bus stop. Together, they waited. They just weren't quite sure for what.

Part II: The Return

Chapter Fifteen

When Isla, Hannah, Shane, Jiao Ming, and Zoe pulled up into the complex on the bus, Isla was pleased to see the same person she'd met on the other side of the border welcoming them to their new home. Taylor Ortiz, the native-born, blue-haired Californian activist around Isla's age, showed Shane his apartment first, a one bedroom big enough for him and, when they freed her, Morgan. Jiao Ming and Zoe shared a two-bedroom apartment on the other end of the hall. Taylor apologized for the lack of space, but Zoe assured them with a smirk that it would be no problem.

Finally, they walked up to the second floor. "Well, Isla and Hannah, this is your room. I live across from you. I'm Taylor, in case you don't remember."

"I remember," Isla said.

Taylor rubbed the back of their neck. "I, uh, if you're comfortable, I'll head out," they said. "I'll get out of your hair and let you settle in. But, you know, if you need anything, I'm here." They jerked their head toward the door across the hall before disappearing behind it. Hannah giggled.

"What?"

"I think they like you."

"Excuse me?"

Hannah grinned and stepped into their new apartment. "This is actually pretty nice." The wall of the living room and attached kitchen area were a pale yellow. Their living room was furnished with a navy couch, two matching chairs, and a coffee table centered over a diamond-patterned rug. The kitchen appeared to have pots, pans, and anything else they might need. They even had a few pantry items.

Isla went to check out her room, painted purple with a twin bed made up with white sheets. Hannah came into Isla's room after a moment. "Mine looks the same," she said. "Do you think the other apartments look like this?"

"Only one way to find out." They locked up behind them and headed down to Zoe and Jiao Ming's apartment, the door still cracked. Hannah peered around the door. "Hey it's—oh, God!" She backed up out of the apartment, covering her eyes. Behind her, the door slammed shut.

"Give us a second!" Zoe called out.

"Fuck, fuck, fuck," Hannah mumbled to herself. "Did you know they were, you know, doing . . . stuff?"

"I mean, I guessed. They weren't exactly trying to hide it. It was pretty obvious."

"If it wasn't before, it is now."

Jiao Ming opened the door, slightly flushed, her shirt rumpled. She cleared her throat. "Sorry about that, Hannah."

"To be fair," Zoe said, coming to stand at Jiao Ming's shoulder, "she did just walk into our apartment."

"The door was open!"

"Whatever. Come in." They did. The two apartments looked pretty much the same, though reversed, since this one was on the other side of the hall.

"Have you reached out to your contacts yet?" Isla asked.

"We just got here," Zoe protested. "Besides, don't get too excited. I know some people at Border Brothers."

"Well, that's good, right?"

"I guess. They don't really do much other than bring people over and help them get settled."

"Oh. But there's got to be—"

"People over here don't really care. Believe me, I've been trying to get them to get their shit together for years. We had better luck with the UN."

"Ok. So . . . let's *start* with Border Brothers then."

That was six months ago. While they'd gotten in touch with Border Brothers, the organization was really only resettling refugees, much to Isla's dismay and Zoe's annoyance. The only people really itching to do more were Taylor and, ironically enough, Faiza Ganesh, the Border Brothers' president, though she wouldn't do anything without the rest of the group's approval.

Finally, they met up with several Border Brothers' volunteers that had quit the organization in favor of doing something more action-oriented. Taylor came with Presley Haugh, a twenty-year-old refugee who'd come to California about a year before their own group. Zoe, Jiao Ming, and Shane sat together, flanked by Faiza, now the former Border Brothers' president, and Parker Ando, Faiza's husband and tech wiz extraordinaire. And the first openly trans person Isla had ever met.

It wasn't much, but still, Isla was grateful for the four of them, that they were willing to risk their safety here for the folks who hadn't managed yet to escape the States, for the people who never would. And she was especially grateful to Zoe, who had talked the other four into joining them.

Faiza, Parker, and Presley were all American refugees themselves at one time, and while they knew what life was like in the States, they weren't necessarily receiving regular updates. Once Isla and the group caught them up on what was happening and why, they were ready to take part.

They were meeting in Zoe and Jiao Ming's rather cramped apartment, but Faiza and Parker said they'd be willing to host future meetings at their place. The group was small, but Isla thought she could work with it. She had no other choice.

She took a deep breath. "Thank you all for coming." She flinched as they all stopped talking, unused to the attention. "Um, we're all here for the same reason. For the revolution." She took another breath and attempted to steady her voice. "So, we have a couple of goals. The big one is to take down Dexter Powers and the system that put him in a position of power in the first place." She glanced down at the notes Hannah had typed up for her at the library. "We hope to free Morgan Young and other political prisoners and establish a government that will benefit the people of the United States. To do this, we'll need to get folks on our side."

For now, their main action item was getting an audience with Powers, something they broke up into several steps. First, they needed to establish themselves as a presence, something Zoe believed they would need more people on their side to accomplish. Isla looked over at Taylor, who was smiling at her, and she felt her stomach warm. Behind Taylor, Faiza's hand was raised. "Yes?"

"How do you plan to get folks on our side?" Faiza asked.

"I got you all here, didn't I?" She didn't mean to sound so dismissive, but Faiza grinned in appreciation, and Zoe laughed.

"I guess you did," Faiza said. "You definitely did."

Isla found the corners of her own mouth creeping up into a small smile. "Good. Well." She glanced over at Zoe, who nodded, and Isla exhaled. "Let's get to it then."

*   *   *

Even before they arrived, Zoe knew California wouldn't be paradise. When California had split from the United States, many of those opposed to the decision migrated back to U.S. soil. But she knew not all of them had. Still, she was increasingly frustrated by the glares she got walking down the sidewalk with Jiao Ming, the sneers they got when they went out to eat. They couldn't be arrested for loving each other, but that didn't stop people from shooting them daggers on the street.

Several days after their first meeting, Zoe was on her way back from the store when a tall man, maybe his mid-forties, stopped her on the sidewalk. "You're the woman I saw the other night, right? At the Red Hat?"

"Oh, yeah. I mean, probably." Faiza and Parker had been showing Zoe, Jiao Ming, and Shane their favorite haunts, including the Red Hat, a downtown bar.

"You were holding hands with that other girl."

Girl? Zoe shifted her groceries to the other arm. "We're adult women, actually."

The man before her frowned, the lines around his mouth deepening. "Get that gay shit out of here," he said. "Or I'll do it myself."

Zoe watched him walk away, swallowing the impulse to call after him. She knew she could take the man out with one hand tied behind her back so long as she had a weapon, but as she didn't have a weapon on her, it wasn't smart to pick a fight with a man twice her size in a country she still barely knew.

Back home, Zoe stormed into the room she shared with Jiao Ming and flopped onto the bed. Jiao Ming, who was reading the Howard Zinn book Isla had lent Zoe, didn't move. "You good?"

"Ugh." Zoe threw her arm over her eyes. She had another headache coming on, this one starting just behind her forehead.

Jiao Ming set the book aside. "What's going on, Zo?"

The compassion in Jiao Ming's voice was almost too much for Zoe to handle. "I'm just sick of being a target, I guess. I'm not going to get arrested or anything here. But I'd like to be able to kiss the woman I love outside a library without being stared at." That specific incident happened just last week.

"Yeah. I know."

"I'm just pissed at myself for getting my hopes up."

"Stop it. This isn't on you. We should be able to love each other."

"I know but—"

"I know you know. I need you to say it."

Zoe rolled her eyes. "Yes, love is love, blah, blah, blah."

"Close enough." Jiao Ming pulled Zoe to her, and Zoe settled her head against Jiao Ming's chest. "I wish it were better here, too," Jiao Ming said.

* * *

"I think we should create a website," Parker said. "To let people in the States know that we're planning on fighting back. And to recruit them."

"We can't put too much on there, though," Faiza said. "I'd worry about Powers and those folks seeing it."

"Just enough to get people invested," Parker agreed. "Let them know there's a cause at all."

"You're going to have to be very careful. And somehow make it so it can't be shut down in the U.S."

"There's a virus I can experiment with that would make it virtually impossible to erase."

"Great, so Parker can work on that," Isla said. She looked around the kitchen table. They were at Faiza and Parker's place, a two-story house about a half-hour walk from the refugee housing complex. "Anything else?"

Parker spoke again. "We have reports from our mole in Powers' office that he suspects someone is spying, but he doesn't know who. If she's willing, I'd love to have Hannah work with me on our next phase."

Hannah pointed at herself. "Me?"

"We'll be planting false letters, memos and such to mislead the president," Parker said. "I hear you're pretty bright when it comes to science and tech."

Hannah blushed. "I'm ok."

"She's brilliant," Isla said. "She'll work with you. What else?" When no one answered, she said, "Alright. Great work everyone." Taylor came into view as they all rose out of their seats, and Isla studiously avoided eye contact with them.

It wasn't as difficult as she thought to distract herself from thoughts of Taylor. Her mind was elsewhere: on the people they left behind in the U.S. Why would they rally behind their little group, especially if they were acting from California?

This was the first time Isla contemplated the possibility of going back. It wasn't an if; it was only a matter of time.

As soon as the others scattered, Zoe dropped down into the seat next to Isla. "How are you doing, boss?"

"I'm not your boss, Zo."

"Yeah, but you're in charge of," she waved her hands in the air, indicating all of this.

Isla didn't know whether to laugh or panic. Sure, she'd kind of stepped up in terms of organizing, but she wasn't so important that the whole movement in California would collapse without her.

Right?

To Zoe, all she said was, "I'm ok."

Chapter Sixteen

Everything hurt. Morgan's skin. Her muscles. Her heart. The only relief from the fever that had been plaguing her for at least a week was lying on the cold, dusty floor, and that probably wasn't great for whatever it was that needed to work its way through her body. The last time she was this sick was when the drugs she'd been given after a knee surgery totaled her immune system.

Someone slammed a door in the distance, and Morgan groaned. That meant someone was coming down to see her, and she didn't particularly feel like seeing anyone.

Christian Shore slammed the door open, sending a fresh wave of pain through her head. She winced and pushed herself into a sitting position against the wall. Christian gave her a once over. "You look like crap," he said.

"Thanks." The one word scratched at her throat and forced her to cough, hard. Christian waited for her to stop before he said, "Really. Is there anything I can do?"

"Ha," she croaked. "I'm good on help from you."

Christian's eyes narrowed. She knew he must be taking in her appearance, her pale skin and red eyes. The whole room smelled like sweat and dirt. They only let her shower when one of the guards complained.

"Water?"

She never got something for nothing. "Why are you helping me?" she demanded.

Christian hesitated. "We want you to give us information," he said. "We don't want you to be sick."

Bullshit. "Do you know what happens if I give you information, Sergeant Shore? They kill me. The captain—that's your father, right?—he'll get rid of me as soon as he can. That's why they killed Mayaan and Arnie. They didn't know enough to be useful—" Morgan cut herself off with more coughing. She leaned forward, her shoulders shaking. Every word was like sandpaper on the inside of her throat.

"That's not true," Christian said. "That isn't . . . ."

Once she'd remembered how to breathe again, Morgan met his eyes. "Are you telling me you didn't know they killed our friends?"

"They didn't," he said. But Morgan could tell he was beginning to doubt himself. Could he really not have known? Or maybe he was lying to himself.

Morgan doubled over again, intermittently hacking and gasping for air. Christian bolted from the room, returning after a minute or two with a glass of water. He set it on the floor just past the bars. The flickering light gave the impression that the water was still moving.

"If you need it," he said, before turning on his heel and leaving Morgan alone.

She eyed the glass warily. She supposed if he really wanted to kill her, there would be easier ways. Slowly, she raised the glass to her lips and took one slow sip and then another. The water was cold and soothed her burning throat. She took another gulp and bent over again, this time gagging. She forced a deep breath. *Breathe in. Breathe out. Slow down.*

Morgan set the glass aside and closed her eyes. In moments, she slid into an uneasy fever dream.

*   *   *

"Come in." The door opened, and Taylor poked their head into Isla's living room.

"Just me," they said. "Still want me to come in?"

Isla was outlining next steps for after they somehow managed a meeting with the president. She was envisioning what they would need to create a democracy that worked. She set the documents she was studying aside. "Yeah, of course. I think Hannah went with Presley somewhere. So, you know, it's just me, too."

"Cool." Taylor returned her grin with a crooked one of their own. "I was hoping to catch you alone."

Isla's heart fluttered in her chest. "Really?"

"Yeah. I was wondering if you'd maybe want to hang out later. Not here, obviously. Like, go out."

"Like on a date?"

Taylor flushed. "Yeah, like a date."

"Yeah. That sounds good."

"Awesome." They hovered in the doorway a bit longer. "Well, how about I come by here around seven o'clock? We could go to this really cool Chinese place downtown."

"I'd love that."

"Ok. Sure. Yeah. Well, bye, Isla."

"Bye." Taylor left, and Isla held a couch pillow to her chest, wanting to hold onto this feeling.

The cool Chinese place, as it turned out, was a little hole in the wall that served mostly lo mein and rice dishes, but it was fairly authentic, Taylor assured her, and Isla really wasn't there for the restaurant anyway.

She wasn't sure yet if she felt anything toward Taylor that was more than just a crush, but if Isla was being honest with herself, she liked being liked. She liked how it felt to be wanted. Before Taylor, she wasn't sure it was a possibility for her.

"So how are you liking California?"

She swallowed her vegetables. "More now that I feel like we can do something," she said. "And more now that I have actual friends here. Presley and Parker and—"

"Me, I hope."

Isla cleared her throat and stabbed at her noodles. "Yeah. For sure." Really, she hoped they could be more than friends.

They went for a walk after dinner, Taylor bombarding her with questions about her life back home, her family, her time here. "Well, what about you?" she finally asked. "You're asking all these questions about me."

"Yeah, because you're really interesting."

Isla blushed, positively reeling. Her, interesting? She had never thought of herself that way. And if she was shaken then, Isla's heart positively soared when Taylor took her hand in theirs.

She tried to think of a question, any question. At last she asked, "Do your parents live around here?"

"Yeah. I go over there all the time. My mom was actually a refugee, too." Taylor paused, seeming to grapple with something Isla couldn't see. At last they said, "She doesn't know what's going on, most of the time. She has dementia."

"Oh." Shit, why did she have to ask? Why was she so bad at this?

"I don't know all the details, but I know she was attacked before she left the States, and it caused a bunch of brain damage. I asked why once, but my dad wouldn't tell me. She started forgetting things when I was five."

Isla's stomach churned. "That's awful."

"Yeah. I know she still loves me, though. Every once in a while she'll remember who I am, and she'll get really happy. She just lights up, you know what I mean?"

"Wow." She wondered what it would have been like to grow up with one of her parents not knowing who she was. The thought made her chest hurt.

"Did your parents accept it when you came out to them?" Taylor asked. Their finger ghosted the back of Isla's hand, sending chills up her arm.

No one had ever asked her that before. "Yes and no. They didn't really understand it, honestly, but they did their best. They tried. And they always made me feel validated. What about you?"

Taylor shrugged as they rounded the corner. "My dad and Parker are friendly, so it's not like he didn't know anyone who's trans. He said he didn't want life to be harder for me, but he was still supportive."

"Yeah." Isla studied Taylor's profile, the slant of their hazel eyes, their candy-blue curls. "Why blue hair?"

Taylor laughed. "Why not?" they asked.

The two of them arrived back at the apartment far too soon for Isla's liking. "Well, um, g-goodnight," she stammered.

"Goodnight." Taylor leaned in, and Isla found herself

frozen, unsure of what to do next. Luckily, Taylor did. They kissed her lightly, like a butterfly landing on her lips. They pulled back, and Isla bit her lip, fumbling for her keys. "Um, right. S-see you." They grinned at each other, and Isla slipped into her apartment. Luckily, Hannah was already in her room. She would tell her sister everything come morning, of course. But for now, she wanted to lie in her own bed, look up at the ceiling, and think of Taylor.

*   *   *

In his search, Adam delicately opened and shut the drawers in Jackson Shore's office, using a paper clip to open locked drawers. He knew he had an hour before the captain came to work, and Adam intended on using every second of it wisely.

It might not even be here, he thought, opening the top drawer of Shore's desk and rifling through papers. He might have it with him, or . . .

Familiar names caught his eye. He took the sheet out carefully, marking its place with the paper clip. They looked like adoption papers from twenty years before. And the names on the document were Morgan Young and Shane Wilson.

Adam frowned. He didn't know Morgan and Shane had a kid, much less a kid they'd put up for adoption. Unless these papers were fake? But why were the edges burnt? And why did Jackson Shore have them?

He glanced at the clock. Five more minutes gone. Shit.

After another twenty minutes, Adam found what he was looking for. Carefully, he separated one key from the others: a small, brass one. Then he left Shore's office, locked the door behind him, and ran.

He was going to make this right. For Morgan.

For the first time in two weeks, Morgan woke without a raging headache, though her chest still burned as she breathed. She sat up slowly, not wanting to risk that changing. Then she realized she wasn't alone.

Morgan leapt to her feet and immediately staggered backward. She leaned against the wall for support and glared at her visitor. "What the fuck are you doing here?"

Adam wrapped his fingers around the bars of her cell. "I'm going to get you out."

"Really?" she smirked. "Feeling guilty? Realized you were a pile of human shit?"

"Yes." Adam averted his gaze, choosing instead to study the filthy floor of Morgan's cell. "I have to do something," he whispered.

She coughed, but not as hard or as long as before. She cleared her throat after and said, "You've already done plenty."

"Did you know you were the only person who ever saw me?" Adam asked, finally meeting her eyes. Morgan said nothing, just glared at him, so Adam said, "My parents viewed me as their protégée. And then when I joined the revolution, I was only as good as the number of bodies I took across the border. But you saw me as a friend."

Morgan scoffed. "Yeah, my mistake."

Adam put his hand through the bars and held out a small, brass key. Morgan stared at it for a moment before she found her voice. "Is that—"

"For your cell," he said. "There's a door up the stairs, to the left. Wait ten minutes after Smith brings you breakfast.

That's the skinny, white guy with the freckles. I'll make sure the door is unlocked and the cameras are off. And I'll leave clothes outside, too."

Morgan took a deep breath. Her legs trembled beneath her as she reached out and grabbed the key from Adam's palm. "What about you?"

"What about me?" He retracted his hand, clinging again to the bar.

"You don't think they'll realize you were the one who helped me?" she asked. "You're the first person they'll suspect."

"I know," he said. Morgan's eyes were still a bit hazy with illness, but there was a determination there. And a concern that sent his heart into a fritz.

"Ok." She stepped back again, leaning against the wall and putting her face back into the shadows. He waited, but she didn't say anything else.

"Ok. Well, take care." He left then, closing the door slowly behind him, hoping she would say something, anything. She never did.

*   *   *

Morgan ran for a solid hour before letting herself slow down and catch her breath. She was coughing again, and she was dizzy enough that she knew she'd better slow down.

It was cold, much colder than it was when she'd escaped last with Shane and the girls. She didn't have anything with her, either. Not even her backpack. Just the clothes Adam had gathered for her: a jacket, a hat, and a scarf. Somehow, she would have to find food.

She pressed on, stumbling along the path framed by sparsely

decorated trees. Twice, she took note of deer watching her, their eyes wide and legs ready to bolt. The bitter air scraped at the still visible skin on the top half of her face and her reddening hands.

After walking a bit further, the sun began to set, and she curled up against the base of a skinny birch tree, hoping she would at least stay warm enough to not get hypothermia as the weather got worse. With that thought, she drifted off into an uneasy sleep.

Chapter Seventeen

Isla could see the surprise on Presley's face when she asked, "The what?" Presley repeated, "The Police Powers Act . . . you all don't know what that is?" Across the table, Shane exchanged a look with Zoe. Jiao Ming just shook her head. The nine of them were once again in Faiza and Parker's home. Parker's site had gone live earlier that day, and try as they might, Powers and his team weren't able to take it down.

"Oh boy," Faiza muttered, rubbing the back of her neck. "You all must have been already on the run then? When it was announced?"

"I barely watch the news, and I know what it is," Presley said.

"Well what is it?" Zoe pressed.

Presley briefly glanced at Shane, then looked away. Faiza spoke instead. "Powers gave the Militum the power to kill revolutionaries," she said. "Of course they've been killing us for forever, but they can do it publicly now. And send messages to more than just the families."

Shane visibly paled. "Send messages?"

Isla's eyes went back and forth, ping-ponging between the others as they spoke. This meant Powers could use Morgan for something other than information. That if he played his cards right, a public death could work to his advantage.

Isla clenched her fists. She needed to talk to Shane after this. If nothing else, this would make him see that they needed to return. For Morgan.

*   *   *

"Adam Boeck. Meet me at padded cell number twelve."

Adam jumped at the voice over the loudspeakers. Morgan had been gone for two weeks now. Shore was furious, but somehow he didn't seem to suspect Adam, who had waited on tenterhooks all week to be punished, perhaps even killed. Dare he believe he'd gotten away with it? If he did, what did that mean for him? What did he do now?

For the moment, he abandoned the break room and went to meet his boss. Adam stepped inside the cell and glanced around. Shore wasn't there yet, but—

CLANG! The cell door slammed shut, and Adam jumped again, every nerve alert. He glanced up at the camera. Was he being watched? "What are we doing here, Captain?" he yelled.

Shore's voice came over the loudspeaker again, confirming Adam's theory. "We needed something to break your fall."

A sudden wretched combination of buzzing, whining, and screeching filled Adam's whole head, bringing him to his knees. Adam grabbed at his head, willing it to stop. Somewhere close, Shore said, "Did you think we didn't know? You were the only one stupid enough to set Young free. Don't worry, though. We'll find her."

The speakers stayed on as Shore projected the sound into Adam's cell. He fell onto his side and curled up into a twitching ball, wondering how much of this he could endure before he went insane.

Christian didn't learn what happened with Adam for three days, how his father had rigged the cell Adam resided in to ring at a frequency that would drive him to madness. When Christian found out, he asked Jackson why.

"He betrayed our cause," Jackson said. "He set Morgan free."

"But you can't know that. It could have been someone else." They were sitting at the dining room table at Jackson's place, preparing to eat dinner. They sat on opposite ends, several feet between them.

"Son, be reasonable. Who else would have done it?"

Christian sat back. He supposed his father was right, that there was no one else with even secondary access to Morgan that would have set her free. But why did that make him uncomfortable? "Do you think this is what he deserves though?" Christian finally asked.

Jackson shrugged. "He won't betray us again. That's for sure."

* * *

Isla sighed and put her head in her hands. "Ok. Five-minute break, everyone."

Faiza and Parker spoke in low voices at the other end of the table. Hannah, Shane, and Taylor, exchanged notes beside Isla, and Presley played on her phone.

Isla put her hands over her eyes. How the hell were they supposed to get anything done from California? How were they supposed to save Morgan? Unless they were in the country with more than just nine people, there was no reason for Powers to listen to them.

She stayed in that position for a minute or two, until she heard Zoe drop into the chair beside her. "It's not enough," Zoe murmured.

Isla felt a surge of appreciation for Zoe, who seemed to understand. She might not use the same words as Isla, but Zoe would agree. Maybe now was the time to bring it up? Tensing her shoulders, she said, "I think we need to go back."

The descending silence was so heavy it was palpable. Jiao Ming looked over at Shane, then at Hannah. Both of them were looking down at their feet. Isla had mentioned this to both of them before, and neither wanted to have this conversation, even after Faiza explained what was at stake.

"You want us to go back?" Jiao Ming asked. "To the States?"

"We're too far away," Isla said. "We need to take the current administration down, but we can't do that from here. We have to bring our demands to the people in power."

"How are we even a threat though?" Hannah said. "We ran. They chased us out."

"Because we were alone before," Isla said. "But we've identified a few people we can work with in the States already. Imagine how many more will want to join us."

Hannah frowned and began to speak, but someone else got there first. "She's right." They all turned to look at Presley, now standing, too. "I'm tired of running," she said. "I'm tired of bringing people over here when they shouldn't have been chased from their homes in the first place. The more of us that leave, the fewer of us there are to fight back on the ground. And they know that."

"I agree," Zoe said. Then she smiled for the first time in weeks. "Let's get these fuckers."

*   *   *

Just like that, the buzzing was gone. Adam pushed himself up off the floor until he was sitting. He shook his head from side to side, certain that something in his brain must have snapped loose at this point. Had it been a day? A week? He wasn't sure anymore. His whole body twitched. There was a dark, wet spot on the crotch of his pants.

Outside the door of his padded cell, heavy footsteps echoed down the corridor. Christian crept into the room as quietly as he could. "I can't keep it off for long," he said. "Just a few minutes."

He reached for Adam, who flinched back. "What are you doing?"

"S-sorry. You have some, uh, blood. Your ear."

Adam felt the sticky wetness on the side of his head and wiped it away with a shaking hand, smearing it onto his fingertips. "Oh." He eyed Christian, still wary, and Christian gave him a small, sad smile. "It's ok," he said. "I wouldn't trust me either."

"Starting to have regrets?"

"Not . . . no, not regrets." What was he feeling, exactly? He didn't think it was regret. Could he regret the pain he'd unknowingly caused? He'd always thought of his cause as justified, but if that was true, why all the lies?

But really, he had known. When his father and the others left for Mayaan's, he could have guessed what they would do and why. He just didn't want to.

"J-just not cut out for this life?" Adam asked, shaking

Christian from his reverie. Adam's words were harsh, but his tone was knowing.

"I guess I've just never known anything else," Chris said. "This has been everything I've known since I was two years old."

Adam frowned. "Why two?"

"I was adopted," Chris said. Then he grimaced. "This probably isn't—"

"How old are you?"

"Oh, uh, twenty-two."

He watched Adam's eyes widen, his brows narrow in thought. "What?" This time, it was Chris' voice that yanked Adam back to reality.

"Did you ever meet your b-biological parents?"

"No, I. What does this have to do with anything?"

"When I was snooping through your dad's stuff to find a key for Morgan, I found these h-half-burnt papers. Adoption p-papers."

"No. It was a closed adoption."

"I don't know what that means. I can tell you the names on the paper though were Shane's and Morgan's."

"Mor—Morgan Young?" A pause. "What do you mean?"

"I think . . . you just look a lot like both of them. I don't know. Maybe I'm cra—"

"You sick fuck!" Chris stood, now towering over Adam. "You just want to get inside my head now?"

"No! I just—"

Chris lashed out with his foot, kicking Adam squarely in the nose, spilling more of his blood onto the already stained floor. "Fuck you," he spat. He turned on his heel and dashed away, back to the control panel. He hit the switch that would restart the horrid noise and hovered there, still breathing hard, tears pricking the corners of his eyes. He could hear Adam's screams reverberating from down the hall. This time, the burning feeling in his belly was almost certainly regret.

* * *

She could deny it all she wanted, but Morgan needed a doctor or at least medication. Every step made her brain ache. She struggled to take each breath. Her knee was so swollen that walking was difficult. She could see her breath in the crisp air, and yet she was flushed and sweating. Whatever progress she'd made in getting better had clearly been undone.

After nearly an hour of stumbling blindly through the woods, she sat back against a tree to catch her breath. Fine, I can at least stop by a pharmacy, she thought. She didn't have any money, and it's not like she had a prescription anyway, but she was positive she could manage to at least take one thing of aspirin without getting caught. Or pretty sure.

Another half an hour later, she'd managed to find a small town. She suppressed a coughing fit while she asked a cyclist at a red light directions to the nearest pharmacy, grateful that Adam's change of clothes disguised her status as a fugitive, even if she still looked a mess. The pharmacy itself turned out to be rather large, with multiple aisles of over-the-counter medication. That would make it easier to remain unnoticed.

She scanned the various medications on the shelves, pulling her wool-lined jacket tightly around her. She was cold now, and chills racked her body. She turned to cough into the crook of her elbow, so hard it made her dizzy. Several shoppers gave her dirty looks, but she hardly noticed.

The dizziness intensified, and Morgan staggered back. She reached out for the shelf in front of her but missed, and then she was falling. She hit the ground on her left side, her knee bursting with pain. Somewhere in the distance, someone shouted. Someone else leaned over her, asked her if she was alright. Then she blacked out.

First, she heard the beeping, low and constant. Second, she smelled the hospital-grade antiseptic. Third, she felt the cool metal cuff cutting into her wrist.

Morgan opened her eyes just a crack. She was definitely in a hospital, and her right arm was definitely handcuffed to her bed. Out of her left arm came an IV with what she assumed must be fluids and probably antibiotics. There were tubes going up her nose. A nurse came in then, setting a clipboard on the table beside Morgan's bed.

"Oh good. You're awake."

Yup. Great. Morgan swallowed and asked, "How long have I been out?" Her voice was low and hoarse. Speaking at all burned her raw throat.

"Shh, don't try to talk. You've been out for three days now. You fainted at the pharmacy."

Ignoring the nurse's instruction, she asked, "The handcuffs?"

The nurse suddenly appeared very interested in the threads of Morgan's thin hospital blanket. "Captain Shore will be here soon." Then the nurse left, leaving Morgan with a chill that had nothing to do with her illness.

She fell into an uneasy sleep for the next few hours, until a *WHACK!* next to her ear startled her awake. Jackson Shore hovered over her, a sick grin on his face. "Welcome back, Ms.

Young."

Morgan wanted to scream, to rail against Captain Shore until she didn't have a voice, to make him hurt the way she was hurting. Instead, she pushed herself up onto her elbows, then immediately fell back, panting. She was still so dizzy.

"You'll keep treating her, right?" That was a nurse, one Morgan hadn't met before, standing at Jackson's shoulder. Morgan knew they couldn't stop Jackson from re-arresting her now, but clearly they thought it was a terrible idea.

"Mmhmm, yes." Jackson checked his watch. "Please discharge her within the next hour. I will be waiting in the hall." He left, and the nurse followed close behind.

Chapter Eighteen

There was no reason for Christian to check. Adam Boeck was a liar. He had already betrayed them. Why would he trust Adam to help him? But it also couldn't hurt to be sure. He snuck down to his father's office after the elder Shore left for the day, first disabling the cameras, then picking the lock, thinking all the while of how Adam must have done the same thing.

"Alright, alright," he mumbled to himself. It wasn't a very large office, so he supposed he would just have to start with the filing cabinets and work from there.

And hope he didn't find anything.

So he did. He went through the cabinets, methodically checking every page, and then he did it again. He checked the tops, but there was nothing there at all. Then he checked the desk.

The drawers were locked, but Chris maneuvered his bobby pin until the lock popped open. And there, in the top drawer, was a half-burnt pile of papers. Quickly, he flipped through them until he got to the page he needed. His name wasn't on them. The adoptee must have been listed on the burnt half, but who else's adoption papers would Jackson Shore have? He flipped frantically through them.

There they were. The names of the biological parents: Morgan Young and Shane Wilson.

Chris was torn between tearing up the papers and flipping the desk. Either would give away his presence, so he did nothing, just stared at the page, trying not to scream. He supposed part of him believed it was a possibility, but how could it be true? Morgan and Shane were rebels. Christian was on the side of the law.

A fleeting thought: But that didn't make his side right.

Voices outside the door startled him back into the moment. He shoved the papers back under the stack, locked the drawer, and crept out of Jackson's office. He soon caught up with two officers he didn't know.

"Found her in Arcadia."

"Damn. That's far."

They must have realized someone was behind them, so they turned, and Christian stopped in his tracks.

"Oh, hey, Sergeant," the first man said. "Where'd you come from?"

"Just headed to the kitchen," he said, naming the first room he could think of that happened to be in this direction. "What's this about finding someone?"

"Morgan Young," the second man said. "Apparently they found her."

"They . . . what?"

"Yeah, they're bringing her in now."

Chris pushed past the two officers, leaving them staring after him. He wasn't entirely sure why he was running, but he knew he had to get there. His father stood outside, watching two of his men lead a heavily chained Morgan inside. He approached Jackson, who spotted him walking over. "Oh good. You're still here."

Christian swallowed a frightening thought: His father knew who Morgan was. Instead he asked, "What's going on? How did you find her?"

"She was seriously ill. She went to a pharmacy for medication and fainted in the aisle. The hospital recognized her and called us."

"Where are they taking her? Back to her cell?"

"A small detour first." Jackson followed the men still supporting Morgan, who seemed to stumble every few steps. Chris followed all of them, his breath hitching when he realized they were headed to where his father kept Adam.

The door was open, the buzzing gone. Morgan stopped walking as soon as they entered the room. "What did you do to him?" Chris peered around her and saw Adam lying on the floor, twitching and mumbling to himself. His eyes rolled around in his head, and his right ear dripped a steady stream of blood. If he knew Morgan was there, he didn't show it.

"Nothing he didn't deserve," Jackson said. "But don't worry. We're about to put him out of his misery."

Everything happened so fast. Morgan turned away, her eyes closed as Jackson raised his gun, aimed, and fired. Christian watched in horror as Adam's blood splattered against Morgan's face, as Jackson replaced the gun in his holster with an expression of utmost calm. A wave of nausea nearly overtook him, and he dashed out into the hallway, gagging and retching. The image of Adam's lifeless hand reaching toward Morgan embedded in the back of his eyelids. Christian sank onto the floor and buried his head in his hands.

"C'mon." He heard one of the guards, he didn't know their

names, speak, and then Morgan was there. Her face in a hard, unreadable expression, but for the sparks in her eyes. "I told you," she hissed at him.

Christian looked up and followed her down the hall with his eyes. She turned around one more time, her own eyes finding his this time, the same shade and shape.

Damn. Adam was right.

As soon as she turned the corner, Jackson approached. "Are you alright?"

"Yeah, I, uh, I wasn't feeling well. Before. I think the smell just . . ." He nearly gagged again remembering the stench of gun powder and Adam Boeck's blood.

"Why don't you go home? I'll get someone to clean up the mess."

"Alright."

Jackson put a hand on Chris' shoulder. "I need you to be strong. Can you be strong?"

"Yes. Really. I think I might just have the stomach flu or something," Chris lied. "I've been nauseous all day."

"Alright. Let me know if you need anything." Jackson left, and Christian shut his eyes. The image of Adam's mangled brains danced in his head.

* * *

Parker steadied his camera on his tripod and said, "I can get the video to pop up first thing on people's search engines. So when they look something up about the war or the revolution, they'll see this." Isla, Parker, and Zoe were sitting in Isla and Hannah's living room. Isla had agreed to do an interview after much needling from Parker and Faiza.

Isla glanced up at him from her couch, where she was sitting with Zoe. "You can do that?"

"Oh, when it comes to computers, I can do anything." He called the website Children of the Revolution and planned for it to feature some of their plans, their outline for a better government, and why it needed to change. It would argue for a restoration of democracy and for Powers' removal. It would have interviews with Isla and the others, and an invitation to join them. Zoe squeezed Isla's shoulder and walked out of Parker's frame.

Parker turned the camera on. "Can you tell me a little bit about you?"

Isla shifted in her seat. She crossed her legs one way, then the other. "I'm Isla Logan. I'm eighteen years old, and I'm a refugee from the United States living in California." She took a deep breath. "Earlier this year, I was arrested for conspiring with revolutionaries, which I hadn't done. Ironically, if the Militum hadn't accused me of doing so, I may never have joined the revolution at all."

She grinned at Parker, who smiled back. "Can you tell me why you thought it was the right thing to do?" he asked.

Isla's grin slipped, and she thought of all she had left to say. "The government doesn't care about me. Not one official cares about us. Only about amassing more power. That involves hurting people, and it's wrong." Remembering Morgan's words, she said, "No one should be punished for who they love or who they are. No one should be imprisoned for just living. And that's what the Militum does."

Parker gestured for her to continue, and Isla took a deep breath. "The Militum, they killed my parents. They killed Arnie Rodriguez and Mayaan Tal, who both helped me when

I had nowhere else to turn. I'm fighting for the revolution because I don't want to see any more senseless deaths." She thought of Morgan, trapped in a cell somewhere with no hope of escape. She shuddered. "No more."

"Great. Anything else?"

Isla shook her head. "No."

Parker turned the camera off and put it back in its case. "Awesome. I'll edit it a bit and put it on the website. But you're great, Isla."

Was she? She turned back to Zoe, who nodded. Isla's heart lifted a bit. Zoe's approval wasn't easy to get.

Maybe she could do this after all.

* * *

Powers clicked out of his secretary of war's folder, sighing to himself. He had gone as far as hiring a hacker to search his employees' hard drives, but so far, they found nothing of value. His wife begged him to leave his work at the office, but Powers brought the computer home, digging through the files. She had gone to bed nearly two hours ago now.

Powers leaned back against his chair and frowned. Whoever the mole was, they probably did their communications outside of the office—Oh. Oh! Powers' eyes widened as he clicked through the contents of the last folder. It was all here. Communications with rebels, plans to bug Powers' office, everything.

He'd hoped against hope that this person specifically would be clean. But his own vice president was, in fact, the spy.

Ilana strode up to Dexter Powers' desk, stopping just short of an arm's reach away. "You wanted to see me, Sir?"

Powers ran a hand over his face. The exhaustion from the night before was just beginning to hit. "This stays between us, alright?" Ilana nodded and Powers said, "Sullivan is a double agent."

"Trevor Sullivan? I'm sorry, Sir, I don't understand."

"We found evidence that Vice President Sullivan is consorting with rebels. Well, was consorting with rebels. He was planning on bringing the administration down from the inside."

"I'm sorry, was?"

"I'll need your help with the media, Ilana. The official story is that Sullivan died of a very sudden heart attack. There was nothing we could do. We all grieve his death."

"Understood."

"You'll need to prepare Captain Shore. He'll be taking Sullivan's place."

"Yes, Sir."

"That will be all." He dismissed her, and Ilana scurried away, shutting the door to the office behind her.

Chapter Nineteen

Flying was nothing like Hannah had thought it would be. When envisioning the trip, she forgot to include the throngs of people at the airport and the overcrowded flight. She didn't anticipate the humidity within the plane or how takeoff would leave her inner ear burning and her insides jostling.

"I keep forgetting it's your first time," Zoe said, moving to give Hannah the window seat. "Then I look at you."

"What do you mean?" Hannah asked, sitting down. She wished she were on solid ground again.

"You're so nervous. Tense. Just relax. Nothing bad is going to happen." Zoe gazed past Hannah, at the cloudless sky. "Nothing yet, at least."

Nothing yet. As the plane began to descend, Hannah's fear grew sharper, more solid. They were heading toward the moment that could decide everything.

* * *

Of all the people they could have chosen to lead, Isla was positive she was not right for the job. Still, she sat in the American consulate in Phoenix, California, waiting to meet with the president of the United States. Hannah, Jiao Ming, and Zoe sat to her left, and Taylor and Shane to her right. The others were downstairs, ready to rush to her aid if needed. All she needed to do was press the button on her watch, a gift from Parker.

As soon as their team had decided they would return to the States, they called for a meeting with Powers, though they didn't think it would go anywhere. To their surprise, Powers' secretary wrote back with dates and times Powers could come to California. Zoe theorized that saying yes would give Powers leverage, that the people would view this as him having nothing to hide. Isla didn't like that idea.

The double doors opened, and Jackson Shore strode into the conference room flanked by five of his men. Behind the six of them, two guards were positioned on either side of—

"Morgan!" Shane knocked his chair over as he stood. Morgan was heavily shackled, her hands were completely covered and her feet were chained together, and she was dressed in prison tan with matching slippers. Her dark hair was a tangled mess, her lips were painfully chapped, and she was so pale that the formerly nearly imperceptible freckles across her nose leapt off her skin. Shane continued to look at her like she was the most beautiful woman in the world.

"You must be Shane," Jackson smirked at him. "I'm sure you remember my son?" He gestured to his left. Christian glanced over at Shane and swallowed, hard.

"Where's Powers?" Isla asked, ripping her eyes away from Morgan.

"He couldn't make it, I'm afraid. It seems he has more important things to do than meet with a group of traitors to the state."

That meant . . . what did that mean?

"Then you better relay this to him carefully," Isla said,

turning her shaking hand into a fist. "Surrender now, and we'll forgive all your crimes against this country's citizens."

Jackson tapped his chin twice, clearly feigning thought. "That's a rather thin offer, considering President Powers hasn't committed any crimes."

"Really?" Zoe asked. "Embezzlement. Fraud. Murder. Ring any bells?" From her lap, Zoe produced a pile of legal documents thicker than the table they now sat on. "We happen to have a hacker among us." Jackson Shore froze for a split second, and Zoe sneered.

Behind her hand, Isla grinned. Another point for Parker.

But Shore's face quickly smoothed over, as though nothing had happened at all. "Ah, that does seem potentially damaging," he conceded. "But I have another proposition for you."

"And what is that?" Zoe asked.

"If you surrender," Shore said, "we let you stay in California—"

Zoe snorted. "That's not much of a deal. You can't exactly drag us across country lines."

"I didn't finish," Shore said, holding up one finger to silence her. "If you surrender, we let you stay in California and you can keep the prisoner with you."

They all looked at Morgan, who was shaking her head. "No." Her voice was low and hoarse, but it was still a relief for Isla to hear it. "They won't do that."

"Oh really?" Shore asked. Isla followed Shore's gaze and frowned. He was gazing thoughtfully at Shane, who was still standing. "I don't know that Mr. Wilson agrees with you," Shore said.

"Morgan—"

"They won't," Morgan insisted. "They can't." She began to cough then, hard. Shane's eyes widened a bit in concern, but none of them moved until she was finished speaking, taking shallow breaths with her eyes closed.

To the rest of them, Shore said, "I'll give you all some time to talk it over." He stood. "My men and I will be right outside, so don't try anything foolish." He stood and turned to go.

"Morgan stays," Isla blurted. She felt her cheeks burn as Shore frowned at her, but she tried not to care. "She's one of us. She gets to help us decide."

He thought about it for a moment. Isla could nearly hear the gears in his head turning: If he let her stay, he would be conceding to one of their demands. At the same time, they would be less likely to send Morgan Young back with the Militum if she was in the room. And if they did ultimately make that decision, he could use it against them.

That, Isla realized, was her biggest fear.

"Fine." Shore snapped his fingers, and all of the Militum men moved out. Christian trailed behind and glanced back at the group before he left.

*　*　*

It was Christian's first time seeing Shane with the knowledge that Shane was his biological father, and the experience left him more shaken than he thought it would. He could barely look at the man without seeing his own features reflected back: the slope of his cheeks, the shape of his nose.

He watched Officer Bolentio check his phone while his father gazed out the window. This was a game to them. A game of strategy. And the pawns were the people inside the meeting room.

The thought made Christian dizzy, and he sank onto a bench in the hallway. Bolentio showed Sergeant York something on his phone, and they both laughed. He understood. For so long, Christian hadn't seen their adversaries as real people, either. But that didn't make it right.

Jackson came and sat beside him. "What do you think they'll do, Son?"

He knew Jackson was more stressed by all this than he let on. Against all odds, the messages the rebels, no the *revolutionaries*, had posted on their website were reaching people, especially the videos. First small and then large protests popped up across the country. Christian would never tell his father this, but he'd watched a few of the videos, and he could see why. Some of what these people were saying . . . he'd never known his side was doing such things. He'd never met real people hurt by Powers' position. Until now.

Christian contemplated the door to the room where the revolutionaries were deciding whether or not to accept their deal. "They'll have to say yes, right? Shane Wilson won't let her come back with us."

Jackson thought about it for a moment. "Possibly, though I doubt it." He didn't elaborate.

* * *

Before the door could even close, Shane rushed to Morgan and sat beside her. He put his hands on her face and pressed their foreheads together. They were both crying.

"I'm ok," she rasped. She moved her hands up, seemed

to remember then that they were bound, and dropped them back into her lap. "Really. You can't take his deal."

"I can't let you go back."

Morgan's lips thinned into a tight frown, and she addressed Isla. "You know what the right choice is."

Tears fell down Isla's cheeks now, too. "I'm sorry, Shane."

Shane sobbed, his shoulders shaking. "But—"

"Please," Morgan begged. "Do this for me. Be strong for me."

"This is ridiculous," Zoe snapped. Her shoulders were shaking, too, but with fury. "Why don't we just take Morgan and regroup? We just lie to them."

"We can't lose the progress we made," Isla said. "There will be too many people who take that as a sign of surrender. I . . . I need you with me on this, Zo."

Zoe shut her eyes tight and took a breath. "I can't lose her, too," she whispered.

Isla hesitated. Was it reckless, playing with Morgan's life like this, especially when she was clearly sick? Did this make her like the Militum, thinking of people as pawns? But before she could speak up, Morgan did.

"So win," Morgan pleaded. "I'm sorry I can't help you anymore. I love you all." She turned to Taylor. "Except for you. I don't know you."

Taylor offered her a faint smile. "I'm Taylor," they said. "I think we met briefly before you were captured."

"Either way. Thank you for taking care of my family." Morgan turned to the side then to cough violently into her shoulder.

Shane grabbed her hand, or rather the bonds that covered

them. "Morgan?"

Morgan shook her head, breathing hard. "I'm ok," she gasped. "Don't worry."

Was she, though? Shane hesitated but didn't say anything else about it. "Can we not call them back in yet?" he asked Isla, desperate. "I need more time."

Isla nodded. "Yes." She didn't want them to come back then, anyway. Not ever.

Shane used the pads of his fingers to wipe the tears from Morgan's face. "You're r-really ok?"

"They're not hurting me," she said. Probably a lie, in Isla's opinion. "But I want to hear about all of you." She looked out at them all. "Isla, you're leading a meeting with the vice president of the United States."

Isla managed a small smile. "What choice do I have?"

"You're amazing," Morgan said. "I'm really proud of you."

Praise like that from Morgan once would have floored Isla. Now, she only felt guilty. More thick tears fell into her lap. "I wish it didn't have to be this way."

"I know. I—"

The Militum burst in through the doors once again, Jackson in front. "Have you made up your minds?" Next to him, one of his men yanked Shane away from Morgan and threw him at the wall, where he staggered but stayed upright. Morgan made to go to him when another Militum man blocked her with his arm.

"Yes." Isla looked back over at Morgan who nodded. "No deal."

"Interesting." Shore's eyes jumped from Zoe, eyebrows furrowed, to Shane, who was still leaning up against the wall, his eyes puffy and red. "So you will take full responsibility when she dies."

Isla's mouth went dry and her heart nearly stopped. Shane buried his head in his hands, and Zoe stood, furious. "You're a real piece of shit."

"Be careful, Ms. Ivanova. That is who you are, right? The lesbian?"

It was a threat that he could have her arrested if she ever came back. Or worse. But Zoe didn't break eye contact, and after a beat, Jackson turned away. "Well if that's all." He turned to leave, and the two guards yanked Morgan up by her shoulders. To Shane, she yelled, "I love you."

"I love you, too." He reached for her, watching her until the door swung shut behind her. Trembling, he reached for a seat and sank into it. Hannah went to him and rubbed his back.

Taylor took Isla's hand and squeezed. "It's ok," they said. "You did ok."

Isla bit her lip as the doors swung shut behind Shore and the others. Even now, she wasn't so sure she'd made the right choice.

Chapter Twenty

When Christian's mother died, at least a dozen people came up to him over the course of the funeral. He didn't even know half of them. Still, he accepted their condolences and stood up straight and even managed not to fidget too much with the tie that his father had demanded he wear.

He didn't even cry. He didn't want to embarrass his dad.

That evening, Christian lay in bed and waited. His mother had always been the one to tuck him in and tell him everything was going to be alright, but maybe his father would remember to do it tonight. Maybe then everything really would be ok.

An hour. Two. Christian watched his clock tick away the minutes with heavy-lidded eyes, exhausted from the day, from the fact that it was far past his bedtime. After four hours, Christian finally admitted to himself that his father had forgotten about him, or else didn't care. Only then did he let himself sob.

Christian shook the unwelcome memory away as he waited for Doctor Yi to finish with Morgan. Yi required quite an expensive bribe, it wasn't every day he got asked to do an illegal exam on a government prisoner, but Christian finally managed to get him down to Morgan's cell. Christian expected to fight with Morgan, too, but the journey to California and back left her exhausted and sicker than before. She really just glared at him as the doctor listened to her crackling lungs. Most of her energy went into just sitting up.

With the exam complete, Doctor Yi closed the cell door behind him and pulled Christian aside. "It's not good."

Christian glanced back at Morgan, now half asleep on the dirty floor. Even on the other side of the bars, he could see how shallow her breaths had become. To the doctor he said, "Tell me."

"It looks like she had pneumonia. She isn't contagious anymore, but it did some severe damage to her lungs."

"Is there any way to reverse it?"

He knew the answer before the doctor shook his head. "Not here," he said. "She'd need aggressive treatment. Possibly a transplant." Chris sighed through his nose and handed the doctor the rest of his money, completing the payment. "Thank you."

The doctor nodded and left, leaving Christian and Morgan alone. It was the pneumonia they'd let go unchecked for so long that ravaged Morgan's insides, the sickness she so clearly had and that Chris did nothing about but bring her the occasional cup of water. He hated himself for the guilt that settled on his chest, making it hard to breathe.

But maybe he could do something about it.

*　　*　　*

Why the hell Powers had decided to have a public execution, Jackson Shore didn't know. Even though her execution was perfectly legal, it was already causing problems. The rebels had put up information about the Police Powers Act on their infuriating website, explaining why it was immoral. At first,

Jackson rolled his eyes, thinking they were wasting their time and energy. Then the protests began.

When they all met in the conference room, Jackson, Powers, and the rest of the president's cabinet and Powers' personal secretary, Jackson made his concerns known. "You'll turn her into a martyr," he insisted. "Better to let her die in her cell."

"I'm sending a message," Powers argued. "The rebels need to know that they can't get away with undermining our—"

"So send a message to the rebels. Send them her head, for all I care. Just don't broadcast her death to the entire country. We execute people in private all the time as warnings to their families."

Powers stood. "Shore, you're either with me or against me," he said. "Which is it?"

Jackson didn't say anything else. Powers, now beet red, settled back into his seat. "The execution will be two weeks from today," he said. "And broadcasted on every major news network." He glared at Shore.

Jackson startled when he walked into his office and realized someone else was already there. When he saw it was Chris, he relaxed and took a seat behind his desk, walking around his son to do so. "You know, it's highly irregular for a Militum sergeant to visit the vice president in his office without an appointment, even if the vice president is said sergeant's father."

The comment might have stung, once. Christian stayed standing. "You're going to kill Morgan Young."

"Who said—"

"Your replacement, Captain Hannon," Christian said.

Ah, he would have to speak with Hannon about that. "Yes," Jackson sighed. "But not in a way I approve—"

"Why didn't you tell me you knew who my biological parents were?"

Jackson froze. Only for a second, but long enough that there was no use in lying. "I didn't want to confuse you," he said.

The rage that had held him captive for so long at once narrowed and relaxed its grip. At least now he understood. "You're selfish," Chris spat. "You've always been selfish. You know, when Mom died I hoped, day in and day out, that you would hug me, tuck me into bed, tell me everything was going to be ok."

Jackson's eyes narrowed. "But everything wasn't ok."

"I was eight years old," Christian cried, pulling at his own hair. "I didn't need a military man then. I needed a father."

"I can't change the past."

"You can tell me the truth now, then. Morgan is my biological mother, isn't she?"

"How could you possibly—"

"I broke into your Militum office months ago and found the adoption papers."

Jackson stood, now nearly as apoplectic as his son. "I could strip you of your rank for that."

Christian burst into hysterical laughter. "You won't," he insisted. "You'd never want people to think your prodigal son did something illegal."

Jackson slammed his hands down on the desk. "Watch how you talk to me."

Christian narrowed his eyes. "Goodbye, Dad." He left the

office, hardly hearing his father screaming behind him. Not too loudly of course—someone might be close enough to hear.

Christian took a breath and lengthened his stride. Next stop, prison.

* * *

Morgan's brutal coughing still echoed down the hall that led to her cell. When Christian opened the door, she was sitting on the floor, gasping for breath. She sat up straighter when she realized she had company. "What do you want?" Morgan sounded like she had swallowed gravel. She cleared her throat and spat something bloody onto the ground. It burned.

"Did you give birth to a son twenty-two-ish years ago?"

"Excuse me?" she said. Whatever Morgan expected, it wasn't that. How could he know? What did this mean?

"This isn't a trick."

Morgan looked him up and down. "I did," she said, still unsure if she should say anything at all.

"I, uh, I think I'm your son. No I, well"—he took the folded up documents he'd pilfered and held them out to Morgan through the bars—"the top half is burnt off, but these are my adoption papers."

Morgan snatched the papers from Chris and flipped through them, scanning each page until she arrived at her own name, hers and Shane's. Her hands shook as she handed the papers back to him. "How did you get these?" she whispered. "I didn't even know the child was adopted."

"My father. He must have hired someone to do some digging." Morgan said nothing. Christian stored the papers in his inner coat pocket and asked, "Are you mad that I told you?"

"No. I—" Her breath caught, and she was thrown into another coughing fit. Her shoulders shook with the force of it, and she could do nothing but wait for it to be over.

"S-sorry," she stammered when she could finally force air into her lungs. Her lips were tainted blue in the dim light. She took another few breaths before saying, "I'm not mad. I just didn't expect—"

"You didn't expect your spawn to be a Militum sergeant?"

"Something like that," Morgan admitted. "I really didn't expect to meet you at all." She studied him for a moment. She might have thought he was lying, but . . . "You're built like Shane," she rasped. "Your face."

"Why did you, I mean . . . I don't know what a not awkward way to say this is."

"Why did we give you up?" Chris nodded and Morgan sighed. "It's complicated."

"I get it," he said. "I wouldn't tell me either."

So he was smarter than he let on, then. "You're still my captor, Sergeant."

"I'm not," he said. "I'm quitting."

"You're . . . what?"

"I'm leaving. What the Militum has done, what I've done, it's not right. It needs to stop."

"And you think you can stop it?" Morgan asked.

"I can try," he said.

She wasn't sure yet if she believed him, but she was starting to. She had seen that determination in herself. "Where will you go?" she asked.

"I'll find Shane Wilson and the others. If I can. If they'll have me."

For a moment, her heart swelled with a pride she wasn't sure she was entitled to. "Would you—" She cut herself off again with more coughing, and this time Christian left. He came back after a minute with a glass of water, and she took several slow sips, pausing to catch her breath. "Just give me a minute," she gasped.

Christian waited as she took several not-quite-deep-enough breaths. Shane would take Christian if she asked him to. And her gut told her it was the right choice.

Finally, Morgan said, "Would you bring him a letter? Shane?"

"Yes. I'll get paper." He left again. When he came back, Morgan was slumped against the wall, her eyes closed and her breathing unsteady. Hesitantly, he called her name. "Morgan?"

She blinked her eyes open and Christian held out the paper and a pen. He watched her while she filled the page, pausing every so often to cough or just to take a breath. Out of the corner of her eye, she saw him glance down at his watch. The next guard would come through soon.

"Here." Morgan held out the pen and paper to Christian, who took them back. "Good luck."

Christian hesitated before he asked his last question. "You, um, you don't hate me?"

"You're learning," she said. "I'm a teacher. I like that." Christian laughed, and Morgan's lips twitched into what was almost a smile.

"Ah, well, good luck to you, too," Christian said. Morgan closed her eyes again and leaned back against the wall, listening to his footsteps fade away. She wasn't stupid. After being married to a doctor for two decades, she knew she wasn't long for this world.

She only hoped Christian would be able to do what needed to be done.

Chapter Twenty One

They headed back to the States. One town, a formerly self-described safe haven for undocumented immigrants, wanted to put them up for the evening. Zoe had found them through another revolutionary she knew, once again impressing upon Isla that they'd probably be screwed without her.

The mayor met them in person. "Please, stay as long as you need," she said, handing Isla several key cards in the lobby of a rather grand hotel, decorated with a fountain lobby and gold trim.

Briefly, Isla wondered how anyone could be brave enough to do this, knowing the risks. Then again, she and her friends were doing the same thing. She smiled at the older woman and said, "Thank you, Mayor Joon."

"Eileen is fine. Please let me know if you need anything." She left them in the lobby, where Isla divided up the keys among the group. At last, it was just their original group from California, plus Faiza and Parker's son Kevin, who was five years older than Isla.

"Hannah and Presley can share, Parker and Faiza, Zoe and Jiao Ming. Shane, do you mind sharing with Kevin?" Both men shook their heads. "So that leaves—" Oh shit.

She and Taylor made eye contact, both blushing. They'd

never gone further than kissing before, much less shared a bed. Zoe shot Isla a knowing smirk, turning Isla a darker shade of crimson.

"Well, um, here." She practically shoved the keys into their hands. "So. Yeah." The others began to leave, except Shane, who quickly pulled Isla to the side. "If you're not comfortable with this, we can work something else out," he whispered.

Oh jeez. "I'm . . . good." Shane left with Parker. Isla and Taylor were the only two people left.

Taylor cleared their throat. "Well, let's go see the room, then." Together, they rode the elevator in silence up to the ninth floor and found their room, a gold-plated 904 on the door. Isla hardly noticed the flat screen TV or the bathroom nearly as large as her childhood bedroom. As it turned out, there were two twin beds in this room. So why did she feel disappointed?

"Well . . ."

"So . . ."

They both stopped. Isla spoke first. "What if . . . what if we pushed the beds together?"

"What?"

"I mean, what if we wanted to, you know." She took a breath. "I want to have sex with you, Taylor. I want you to see me. If . . . if you want to."

"Really?" Isla nodded, and Taylor came to her, kissed her lightly on the mouth, then harder. They broke away, both panting slightly, and moved to push the beds together.

Jiao Ming, Zoe, Shane, and Parker were all in the lobby when Isla came down. She had showered and napped briefly in clean sheets for the first time since leaving California. It hadn't been a terribly long trip, but her time escaping the U.S. made her wary. What if they didn't get the chance again?

"How are you doing, girl?" Zoe asked, scooting over on the couch.

"I'm ok," she said, taking a seat. "It's scary to be back."

Zoe nodded. "Yes. It is."

She looked around at the rest of the group, her heart lighter with her love for them. "You're all ok spending another day here? I know it's a risk."

"Yeah," Parker said. "We can do some interviews with people here? With some of the civilians and Mayor Joon?"

"Great," Isla said. "Thank you all."

Zoe put her arm around Isla. "You're doing great," she told her. "We're all here."

Isla nodded, suddenly fighting tears. She hadn't fled the country expecting to find a family. But she did. Now, she couldn't bear to lose a single person.

"Anyway," Zoe continued, "apparently this hotel wants to give us all free snacks, so we were just debating how to best take advantage."

Isla laughed and reached across Zoe to take the menu from Jiao Ming. Hannah, Presley, and Taylor all joined them before long, and for the rest of that night, eating popcorn and cookies with their small group in the lobby of a fancy hotel, she felt like a kid again. For one night, she allowed herself to forget how in danger they all were.

Their group did end up spending another day at the hotel, planning, recuperating, and broadcasting. It wasn't safe to go out much—someone could recognize one of them. So Isla, Hannah, Taylor, and Presley spent much of the following day in Hannah and Presley's room, playing Sails and telling each other stories.

"I can't believe you took a break," Taylor said, staring at Hannah in disbelief. "Adam must have met with the Militum or something."

"In hindsight, it was way weird," Hannah admitted. "But I think we were all just so relieved to have a break."

"The woman who was my guide would never," Presley said. "She was a no-nonsense kind of person."

Hannah fell quiet, listening. It wasn't often she could get Presley to talk about her own journey. Given what Hannah knew already, it wasn't surprising that her friend didn't want to remember.

"How did you find someone to go with?" Isla asked. "I never would have known if not for Morgan."

"I was already running, and I got pretty sick. It was February and freezing. I didn't know where to go, so I just showed up dirty as fuck at a stranger's house, hoping they would take pity on me. He wasn't part of the revolution, but he felt bad and brought me to someone who was."

Briefly, Hannah wondered how many people there were like Presley: already on the run when disaster struck. She wondered how many of them didn't have that stroke of luck that could have saved them.

"Hey, we should see if there are any more snacks downstairs," Taylor said. "Wanna go?" The rest of them agreed, and talk of the revolution was forgotten for a brief and blissful moment.

* * *

Parker was editing footage with Shane in Parker and Faiza's room when he leaned aback against his chair and said, "Just have to wait for it to buffer now. Thanks for your help."

"I didn't do anything."

"It's just nice to have company," Parker said. "Any chance I could get you on camera?"

Shane laughed. "Nah, I'll leave that to the others." No one wanted to see a forty-three-year-old doctor talk about the revolution, anyway.

"Well, if you change your mind, I'm always happy to have you."

"I don't even know what I'd say," Shane said. "There's too much."

"Oh, I hear that. Did you fight in the war, too?"

"Ish. I was a medic."

"Yeah. I spent eight years in the military. Before the war. Ages eighteen to twenty-two overseas fighting in someone else's war and then twenty-two to twenty-four, I fought here. Until the Civil War ended."

Shane whistled. "That's a long time."

"Yes. It was."

"How did you, um . . . forgive me if this is rude—"

"Why am I a refugee?" Shane nodded, and Parker said, "They kept rolling back protections for people like me. I couldn't get a job because I'm trans, and when I did get a job, they could fire me for being Asian. I used to get harassed on the street. There were a few times I feared for my life. A few years ago, I got beat up bad by a bunch of men in the middle of the street in broad daylight, and no one did a thing. I got laughed at when I reported it. I left the next day."

"Oh."

"It's all in the past. Faiza was actually a guide then, and she stayed behind with Kevin so she could keep going. She went back and forth a couple times after that, before she had to make a run for it herself. Honestly, I was terrified for her and Kevin, but so glad when they came over. I hadn't seen them in almost two years."

Shane didn't know what to say. Compared to Parker, his own story came off looking like a comedy. Parker seemed to pick up on this and admonished him. "Don't feel sorry for me. I'm glad I can be doing something about it now, you know?"

"Where did you live?" Shane asked.

"Oklahoma. Close to the border, so it wasn't far to go. I remember being floored when the borders changed. I hadn't realized it was so easy—"

A knock on the door interrupted Parker midsentence. The two men exchanged looks, and Shane went to open it. "Hello?"

A twenty-something in a hotel uniform stood at the door with a tray in his hand. "Room service, courtesy of Mayor Joon."

"That's . . . nice of her." Something about this felt really off to Shane. He just couldn't say what.

The young man entered the room and set the tray down on one of the beds, barely making a dent. That's when it hit Shane. The tray was too light. It was empty.

"Parker, down!" They both ducked as the man took a gun out of the back of his belt and fired, hitting Parker's camera. Shane leapt over one of the beds and tackled the man. He attempted to knock the gun away, but the man held fast, shooting twice more, and Shane heard Parker cry out. The man flipped Shane then so that Shane was below him. He pointed the gun—

BOOM! Shane squeezed his eyes shut as the man's blood splattered everywhere. He pushed his would-be assassin to the floor, the man's eyes wide and empty, a bullet lodged in his brain. Shane sat up and saw Hannah, gun held out front, her whole body shaking.

"Hannah?" Shane got up and went to her. On the floor, Parker sat up and stared, open-mouthed.

"I h-heard shots," she said, lowering the gun. Her eyes were somewhere far away. "Oh God, I killed him. I killed him."

"Hannah, listen, that man was a second away from killing me. You just saved my life."

Hannah set the gun on the bedside table. Then she sat on the bed and burst into tears.

Shane sat beside her and put his arm around her shoulders. "Shh. It's ok. You're ok."

"I thought you were going to die," she sobbed. "Please don't die. No one else can die."

"I'm not going anywhere." He held Hannah while she cried into his blood-spattered sweater and begged him to stay safe. After a moment, still holding Hannah, he remembered Parker. "Are you ok?"

"Yes. One of the bullets grazed my shoulder, but it just stings."

"Could you turn around?" Shane said. Parker did, and Shane saw the wound, superficial and already drying. Thank God.

"I'm sorry," Hannah said, finally wiping her eyes. "I didn't mean to f-freak out."

"It's ok," Shane said. "I get it. You never have to apologize, ok?" He rubbed her arm. "It's late. Can I give you something to sleep?"

Hannah nodded, and Shane grabbed a sleep syrup from his bag. He guided her back to her room and knocked gently on the door. "It's Shane."

"Come in," Presley called, and Shane did. Presley sat on her bed with Jiao Ming. Faiza sat on Hannah's bed.

"What's going on?" Shane asked.

"Eileen Joon is dead," Faiza said. "Kevin just heard. She was shot."

Shane felt the room slipping away, suddenly dizzy as the rush of the day hit him all at once. He stumbled into the wall and brought himself back. "Ok. We have to leave first thing tomorrow." He took a breath. "Zoe knows, right?"

Jiao Ming frowned. "Shane, you're covered in blood."

Oh. Right. He sat at the edge of Presley's bed and explained what happened: the attack, the imminence of his own death. He skirted around Hannah's involvement, but they all seemed to understand.

"I don't think he was specifically there to kill us, though," Shane said. "He shot at Parker's camera first, and it was nowhere near us."

"So he was trying to stop the videos?" Presley asked.

"Looks like it."

"Good," Jiao Ming said, her arm now around Hannah, who was crying quietly.

"Good?" Shane asked.

"They're scared. That means the videos are working."

"You still have the footage?" Faiza asked.

"I think so. Everything from today was on Parker's computer, and the memory card wasn't damaged." He looked down at his bloody clothes again. "I'll shower, and then I can come back to talk plans."

"We can all do that," Faiza said, standing. "You should rest."

He was about to protest when it hit him just how exhausted he was. His whole body felt heavy and distant, like it wasn't his own. "Yeah. Yeah, ok." He handed Jiao Ming the sleep syrup. "For Hannah. One capful." And then Shane left, heading back to his room. He stopped just outside the door and sat against the wall. He heard Parker, newly wounded, stumbling around inside their room trying to salvage what was left of that day's work.

And then there was the body in their room, the man that had meant to end their lives. In the immediate aftermath, Shane had thought, for a fleeting moment, that the mayor betrayed them, only to learn she was killed, most likely for helping them. But this man had to be acting alone, or else they all would have been taken, right? Or was it foolish to think there weren't more coming?

Did Morgan ever feel like he did right then? Did she ever just want to say fuck it and go home? Hell, he thought. He didn't have that choice anymore, anyway. Home was Morgan, and she was gone.

Chapter Twenty Two

After their group left the hotel, they met up with several revolutionaries, people that Zoe, Parker, and Faiza knew. They brought tents and trucks, food and medical supplies. Several of them with experience were designated medics. Others who had experience working with food became cooks. A few offered to drive the tents in their trucks whenever the group moved. They set up a large overhang as a place to eat, and Parker managed to get a few TVs hooked up so they could watch the news. No word of their own activities yet, which they took to be a good sign.

It was in their makeshift mess hall that Shane recognized the sound. The whistling, getting closer, and then a *BANG!* somewhere in the distance. He stood at the table where he'd been eating with Hannah, Presley, Zoe, and Jiao Ming. "That's a bomb."

Zoe put her fork down. "Excuse me?"

"That's a bomb," Shane repeated. "We have to get everyone out of here."

Of course they couldn't have a moment of peace. "And to where?" Behind them, another whistle, another explosion.

"There's a town not far from here. We should go—"

"We can't use civilians as a shield, Shane. You think

Powers won't bomb them anyway? Make it look like we led the destruction right to them? That's what the papers will all report."

"No, I mean they must have basements. And if the town is close enough, the civilians are in danger, too. We need to get them to safety."

He made a good point. Zoe rose, as did the others. "Lead the way."

Shane stood on the table and yelled as loud as he could. "Excuse me!" Heads turned in his direction. "There's an attack coming this way. We need to get into town and get all the civilians into basements, bunkers, anything underground. Go. Now!"

The others scattered. Isla and Taylor came out of the crowd, and Isla grabbed Shane's arm. "What's going on?"

"We're being bombed." Another whistle, closer now. This time, the bang rattled the tent just slightly.

"Ok. Let's go."

They ran, arriving quickly in town, and scattered, hitting every shop and home they could and explaining to civilians that they needed to take cover. Between all of them, they managed to get almost everyone underground in less than half an hour.

"We have to take cover now, too," Shane told them. "Wait for me to give the all clear." The bombs were getting closer now. They were deafening when they went off, and the ground trembled beneath them.

They scattered once again, making sure there were no civilians left before they protected themselves. That's when Zoe came across a small boy huddled outside The Mohapatra Flower Shop. She crouched down in front of him. "Hey.

Where are your parents?"

The boy shrugged. There was no one there. In fact, the entire block was empty. "We need to get underground, ok?" Zoe said. "What's your name?" The destruction would be upon them any minute now.

He blinked up at her. "Kyle."

"I'm Zoe. Will you come with me into the basement until it's safe?"

Kyle nodded, and Zoe took his hand. They entered the shop, and Zoe spied a door, hopefully a basement. She grabbed Kyle's arm and forced him closer to—*please, please let it be the cellar.* "I know it's scary," she said. "But everything will be—"

The force of the next explosion blew up the store.

On sheer instinct, Zoe dove for the boy, knocking him under the desk as their world exploded, glass and debris flying everywhere. Zoe felt a sharp pain against her head, and another at her side. She clung to the boy, covering him the best she could with her own body. The next explosion toppled the desk, bringing it down on Zoe's back. Fierce, blinding pain. Then, nothing.

*   *   *

After nearly an hour of silence, Shane let the others exit their hideout and asked them to go door-to-door, making sure everyone else knew it was over. Not for the first time, Jiao Ming wondered what else the Civil War must have done to Shane and Morgan. He'd recognized a distant whistle as a bomb immediately, before the rest of them even heard it. That couldn't bode well for his mental health.

Several of the shops were blown up along the street Jiao

Ming and Shane took, but there were no bodies; all of the people were underground. When she at last came upon what was formerly a flower shop, Jiao Ming knelt down in front of a young, shell-shocked boy. "You ok, buddy?"

The boy looked at her with wide eyes. "There's someone in there," he said. "A lady saved me."

Before them, the rubble was smoking. Behind her, Shane asked, "Jiao Ming? Did you get them all?"

"There's someone in there," she said, pointing to the shop. "Let's go."

In her head, Jiao Ming ran through everyone on their team, everyone she hadn't yet seen. *What if it's Parker? Or Kevin?* Together, she and Shane stepped between debris and wilted plants, pushing the mess aside in the search for their person. Together, they moved a large desk to the side.

"Zoe!" Jiao Ming knelt down next to the bruised and broken woman, her chest pounding. Zoe stirred, then winced. "Jiao . . ."

Shane knelt beside Jiao Ming. "We have to get you out of here, Zo. Can you stand?"

Blood slowly crusted over Zoe's temples. The whole building smelled of fire and smoke, forcing bile into Jiao Ming's throat. "C-can't feel my legs," Zoe mumbled. She turned her head to the side to cough and spat soot onto the debris.

"I'm going to carry you," Shane said. "Hang on." He and Jiao Ming moved the rest of the debris aside as quickly as they could. When at last she was fully exposed, Shane lifted Zoe into his arms and carried her out of the rubble.

Isla came up to Jiao Ming, who was making her own way out of the debris. Her eyes were wide and panicked. "Is that Zoe?"

It was Zoe. Zoe, whom the revolution relied on. Zoe, who had been so strong for so long. Zoe, whom Jiao Ming loved and who loved Jiao Ming. "She's alive. Sh-she saved a boy." Jiao Ming sank to the ground, tears falling freely. "Fuck!"

Isla crouched so that she could put a hand on Jiao Ming's shoulder. Jiao Ming was shaking now. Her hands covered her face. "Jiao, we have to get out of here, ok? Zoe will be ok, but we have to move."

Jiao Ming wiped at her eyes, but she couldn't manage to stem the flow of tears. She let Isla guide her away from the shop, away from the town. Isla's fear had turned into remarkable stoicism in a matter of seconds, Jiao Ming noted. In some ways, she was frightening in her calm.

Somehow, their camp was mostly unscathed. The only two tents hit were for sleeping, and no one was inside at the time of the blast. Go figure.

Unless it wasn't a mistake. Unless Powers knew they would go save the townsfolk.

Jiao Ming and Isla found Shane in the medical tent. Zoe was being tended to by two volunteers Isla didn't know. She approached Shane. "How is she?"

"She has a pretty serious concussion and shrapnel buried between her ribs," he said. "The most damage is to her back. It looks pretty broken."

"But, she'll live?" Jiao Ming asked.

Shane exhaled loudly. "I think so."

"You think so?" Jiao Ming heard her voice rising with every word, but she couldn't stop herself.

"We'll have a better prognosis if she makes it through the night."

"If?"

"When."

"Jiao Ming," Isla murmured. "She's strong. She made it through so much already. She'll make it through this."

On the bed, Zoe cried out, and Jiao Ming ran over to her. One of the nurses was removing shrapnel from an open wound on Zoe's side, over her ribs. "Can't you give her anything?" Jiao Ming asked Shane.

"No."

Zoe grimaced and winced as the volunteer uncovered a rather large piece of something sharp under her skin. Jiao Ming sat on her other side and took Zoe's hand. "I'm so tired," Zoe moaned.

Shane came up behind Jiao Ming and put a hand on her shoulder. "You can't sleep, Zo. You have a really bad concussion."

Zoe moaned again and gripped Jiao Ming's hand tighter. The other volunteer went by Zoe's head and began to apply bandages there. "Still can't feel my legs," she mumbled. Shane bit his lip and didn't say anything.

Chapter Twenty Three

Christian put his hands up as a vaguely familiar woman pointed a gun at his head from across a clearing in the woods. "Freeze!" He did and then waited for her to approach.

He had found the revolutionaries' camp through word of mouth, people sympathetic to the revolution willing to tell him how he could join their cause. This is how he came to the woods outside of a small town—or what used to be a town. The buildings were all demolished, as though they had been bombed. Christian had a pretty good idea of the why and the how. If people were optimistic enough to believe they wanted to do right by the revolution, it wouldn't have been hard for the Militum to ask around and find the information they needed.

The woman stopped several feet from him. "You're a Militum officer," she said. He realized he recognized her from the embassy. He had passed her on the main floor.

"Not anymore," he said. "Do you know Shane Wilson?" the woman nodded, and he said, "I'm Chris Shore. I have a letter from his wife."

This was how, less than an hour later, Christian found himself in a rebel tent with two guns pointed at his head, one by the woman he now knew to be Presley Haugh. Finally, Shane entered, flanked by Isla and Jiao Ming. Shane held his hand out. "Let's see the letter."

"Ms. Haugh has it," he said, nodding at Presley. She handed the paper to Shane, who held it gently as he stared at the words.

"What did you do to her?"

Chris blinked. "What?"

"This is her handwriting, but it looks like she was shaking. Did you hurt her?"

"No! She was sick. She's still . . . she had pneumonia a few months back and they—we—never treated it. So she's still weak."

Shane's chest rose and fell rapidly as he recalled how ill Morgan seemed at the embassy. "How weak?"

Isla put a hand on Shane's shoulder. "She knows we're coming for her. She'll be ok."

Shane pressed his lips close together. Then he delved into the letter.

Dear Shane,

I'm sorry for the brevity of this letter. I don't have much time, and there are so many things I want to tell you. First, that this letter comes in the hands of Christian Shore. You can trust him. I know you'll be reluctant to, but we need everyone we can get. He's really just a misguided, broken boy who's been fed lies all his life and who needs some guidance. I'm hoping our makeshift family can give him just that.

This is so much to take in, but you have the right to know: Christian is also the baby we gave up for adoption so many years ago. I don't really know what to do with this information, but it's only fair, I think, that we give him the truth. We didn't resent him. We resented our impossible situation, and he had to bear the brunt of it. We resented living in a country that didn't give me the rights to my own body. He can know that and everything else. I trust you completely.

Now, on to the most difficult part. Shane, I love you with my whole heart, and in writing this letter, I know the odds of ever seeing you again are slim. But I need you to keep fighting. Fight for me and you. Fight for Isla and Hannah and Zoe and Jiao Ming. Make a better world than the one we were born into. You can do that because you are the strongest person I know. You, who went to hell and back with me, are the perfect person to change this country. You, along with our friends and allies who share in the same dream.

I do love you, so much, and always will. I'm sorry for whatever might happen. But I know you can get through it.

Yours forever,

Morgan

Shane didn't realize until after he lowered the letter that he was crying. He wiped at his eyes and addressed Presley and Faiza first. "You can lower your guns. He's not a threat."

They both lowered their guns, though Presley pursed her lips as she did so. To everyone Shane said, "Can you give me a moment with Christian?" The others filed out of the tent, Jiao Ming and Isla last. "Yell if you need anything," Isla said. "We'll be right outside." Finally, they were all gone, and Shane turned his attention to Christian.

"Did she, um, say in the letter? That you're my—"

"Yes." Shane ran his finger over the letter, over the words Morgan had written. How was this possible? He swallowed all the questions he had about Christian and asked one about

Morgan instead. "Tell me really. Is she ok?"

"She's . . . not doing well."

"The letter makes it sound like she's dying."

"I don't know. The coughing's really bad, and she's tired all the time."

Shane sniffed and wiped his eyes. He had to focus. "Why did you come here?"

Christian looked up at him with eyes so much like Morgan's it hurt. How had he not seen it before? "I came because it's the right thing to do," Christian said. "I came because my whole life I've been told that the rebels are bad people. And then I started to meet them."

Shane tucked the letter into his breast pocket and went to Christian. "As long as you're willing to fight with us," he said, "we'd love to have you on our side."

* * *

Still half asleep, Morgan forced her eyes open as an unwanted guest snuck quietly into her cell. She sat straight up, feigning control. It was the evening before her execution. "Who are you?" she rasped.

The woman knelt in front of the bars. "My name is Ilana Cruz," she said. "I work for Powers."

Morgan snorted. "Fuck off then." Hadn't they tortured her enough?

"I'm a double agent," Ilana explained. "Working with Parker Ando and Hannah Logan. I'm the one who framed the vice president."

Morgan didn't know what happened to Sullivan. But one name caught her attention. "You know Hannah?"

"Seems like she's a good kid."

Morgan hesitated. "What do you want from me—" She started coughing again, and Ilana slipped a glass of water through the bars. Morgan took slow sips with a trembling hand until she couldn't hold it steady anymore. She set the glass aside.

"Powers trusts me," Ilana finally said. "He's going to have me by his side for your execution. I'm going to fix his mic so that it's recording everything, even before he means it to. When he asks you for your final words, make them count."

Morgan took a moment to process the words. "So that's it? You're not going to tell me there's a secret tunnel out of here, or—"

"No. I would if I could."

"Is it because there's really no way? Or because I'm more helpful to the revolution dead?"

Ilana sighed. "Both."

Morgan nodded. She knew it might come to this eventually. "Ok," she said. And with a small, sardonic smile she added, "I guess I'll see you at my execution."

"I'm sorry, Morgan."

"We all die eventually," Morgan said. "Like you said. Make it count." She handed the half-filled glass back to Ilana, ridding her cell of any evidence of a visitor. Ilana took it and turned to leave as Morgan sat back against the wall, closing her eyes.

Death by illness wasn't enough to win a war. But hanging a woman who couldn't make it ten steps on her own? That just might inspire enough people to turn the tide.

Morgan knew what had to happen. That didn't make it

easy.

The next morning, Morgan woke herself up by coughing blood onto her dingy cell floor. It took her a moment, preoccupied as she was by the pain racking her body, to realize that Jackson Shore stood over her, his hands on the bars of her cell, watching. Christian's father, she thought. No wonder the kid joined the Militum.

"It's a good thing your death is planned for today," Jackson said. "You wouldn't have made it much longer anyway."

Morgan wiped her mouth with the back of her shaking hand. "I know that," she gasped.

"Come," he said. He opened the door to her cell.

"What, no handcuffs?"

"You don't have the energy to fight," Jackson said, reaching out a hand. She took it, and he helped her up. Then he took her arm and led her up the stairs.

Jackson handed Morgan off to the president, who gave her a once over, as though assessing whether this waif of a woman was truly the rebel who had given them so much trouble. The same rebel who somehow broke out of prison and killed a dozen Militum men. The same rebel that took dozens more across the border. The thought nearly made her smile.

"Do you have any last words, Ms. Young?"

This was it. She leaned in close, blood still on her lips. "You kill people who oppose you because you're afraid of losing power," she rasped. "But my husband will keep fighting. My family will keep fighting. Because we care about the people of this country. We don't fight because we're afraid to lose.

We're fighting because we love this country and you're letting it burn."

She heard murmurs throughout the crowd, and Powers looked out, startled. Morgan watched him look down at his mic, flashing green to signal it was on. The sound booth, where Ilana had been, was now empty.

He covered the microphone with his hand and leaned toward the sergeant beside him, positively irate. "Find Ilana Cruz and bring her to me when this is over." The man nodded, and Powers turned back to the matter at hand. "Morgan Young, you are sentenced to die for your crimes of domestic terrorism and murder." He took her so roughly by the arm she nearly fell over and led her up the stairs, to the noose swinging in the breeze.

*   *   *

"Shane!" Shane and Jiao Ming turned from Zoe's bed, where they had been visiting until Zoe fell asleep.

Shane stood up as Presley approached them. "What's going on?" he asked.

"Come." Presley ran out of the hospital tent with Shane and Jiao Ming hot on her heels. They went into the tent Parker used for his broadcasting. On the large TV on the opposite wall, Morgan stood beside the president. The text at the bottom of the screen marked the event an execution.

"No," Shane whispered, approaching the screen. "No!"

Isla went to him, but he shook her off. They were so close. There had to be a chance. On the screen, Powers said, "Do you have any last words, Ms. Young?"

Morgan leaned in close to him. "You kill people who

oppose you because you're afraid of losing power. But my husband will keep fighting. My family will keep fighting. Because we care about the people of this country. We don't fight because we're afraid to lose. We're fighting because we love this country and you're letting it burn."

Presley, now seated between Hannah and Christian, asked, "Were we supposed to hear that?" Shane barely heard her.

Faiza, standing behind Shane and Jiao Ming, shook her head. "That was Ilana, our spy in the president's office. She made a run for it just now."

Shane didn't hear her. He watched two officers come forward, sling the noose around Morgan's neck and tighten it just enough so that it would end her life. And he watched as the floor opened up beneath her, doing just that.

Part III: The Revolution

Chapter Twenty Four

The drugs they gave Morgan after her third knee surgery totaled her immune system for weeks. In the aftermath of the surgery, she slept for hours on end and woke up still tired. Twice in three weeks, she was confined to bed after an illness knocked her off her feet. The second time, it was strep. Her throat was so swollen she struggled to get enough air with each wheezing breath.

When finally, after six days, she felt well enough to get up on her own, she wandered into the living room and burrowed under the blankets on the couch beside Shane. He set aside the text he'd been studying for class and pressed his lips to her forehead. "No fever," he murmured.

"I'm hoping this is the last one," she sighed, leaning her head against his shoulder. Her voice was still hoarse, almost raw, but that was the most Shane heard her speak in almost three days.

"Me too. How are you feeling?"

"Not as tired as before," she croaked. "Still a little achy." She lifted her head, and Shane saw the freckles splashed over her nose, the light in her eyes. "What?"

"Nothing. You're just beautiful."

"I smell like sweat."

"You're still beautiful."

"My hair is a mess."

"A beautiful mess."

Morgan grinned. "You're such a dork."

Shane had thought of about a million ways to propose to Morgan. At the restaurant where they had their first date. On the trip they were planning to Cairo when he graduated med school. And as much as this would have seemed like a terrible time to an outsider, to Shane it felt right. He slid off the couch and knelt before her. "Morgan—"

"Oh my God. Are you really doing this now?"

Shane took a small, white case out of the drawer beside the couch. He had moved it around their home a million times since he'd gotten it, just wanting to hold it, to anticipate Morgan's answer. "Marry me?"

"Yes. Yes!"

Shane grinned and opened the case. He slid the ring onto Morgan's finger, still beaming, and put his hands on either side of her face. He kissed her hard, pouring everything he had into letting her know just how much he adored her, how he could never again live without her.

*　*　*

At first, Isla could only hear the overwhelming buzzing in her ears. They did it. They fucking did it. Those words repeated in her head like a mantra. Of all the horrors she had experienced at the hands of this regime, she somehow convinced herself they had a chance to save Morgan.

Then the noise cleared, and all she could hear were Shane's screams.

He was on his knees, shaking all over. Hannah went to him, also sobbing, and wrapped her arms around him as best she could. Jiao Ming joined them on the floor, rubbing Shane's shoulder and whispering words he didn't seem to hear. Christian stared, openmouthed, at the screen. Presley and Faiza, likewise, looked stunned.

Isla ran from the tent, Shane's screams following her far beyond it. She ran until she reached the mess hall, where she knew Parker usually was this time of day—he went there after he finished a morning's worth of editing. She ran to him and Kevin, who were both staring at the TV overhead. Jackson Shore appeared to be speaking to a reporter.

Kevin noticed her first. "Isla—"

She ignored him. "I need to send a message," she told Parker. "Can you help me?"

"Y-yes." He glanced back up at the TV, looking faintly ill.

"Now."

Parker stood. "Of course." He followed her out of the mess hall, back to the electronics tent to grab his equipment. Shane was outside now, Hannah on his left and Jiao Ming on his right. She didn't see Christian. The others, Isla knew, had never met Morgan. She would leave them be unless they were needed.

Isla knelt down in front of Shane, who was trembling violently. "I'm sorry," she said. "I'm so—"

Shane brought his arms around her, enveloping Isla in a hug she didn't think she deserved. It was her fault Morgan was killed. She'd made the wrong call. And she would live with that knowledge forever.

As though he could read her mind, Shane whispered, "This isn't your fault. It isn't. It's th-theirs." He pulled away, swiping at his tears with the palms of his hands. "I j-just c-can't—"

Jiao Ming leapt out of the way just as Shane leaned over to retch. Hannah took hold of his arm and kept him steady until he was done and then gripped him by the shoulder. "We should get you to medical," she said, her voice shaking.

Shane didn't say yes or no. He didn't say anything. But he did take Hannah's hand when she offered, and he left with her and Jiao Ming, leaning heavily on both their shoulders. When Isla regained her composure, she remembered Parker was there.

She turned around to face him and took a deep breath. "Ready?"

Parker nodded, his hands trembling as he raised his camera. The on light lit up, and Isla took a breath. "Today, I lost a mentor, a teacher, and a friend. Morgan Young was part of the revolution, but she was also so much more than that. She was a wife, and a friend, and . . ." Isla closed her eyes tight. She was repeating herself.

Deep breaths. It's ok. This is good. She opened them again and let the tears fall. "Morgan was willing to die for us, for all of us. I doubt that Dexter Powers cares about any one of us enough to make the sacrifices Morgan made or that so many of us will have to make. He isn't fit to lead us, and he needs to be stopped before anyone else has to die." Parker lowered the camera. "Was that ok?" Isla asked.

Parker had tears in his eyes, too. "Yeah, Isla. That was perfect."

*　　*　　*

Though the pain in her side still plagued her and she was still occasionally overcome by vertigo, Zoe's biggest concern was the numbness in her legs. It had been two weeks, and she still couldn't feel anything below her waist. In all that time, they hadn't moved camp. Zoe wondered what she would do when they did.

She heard the flap open and looked over at the entrance of the tent. Shane stumbled in, half supported, half dragged by Hannah and Jiao Ming. They sat him down at the edge of a bed, and Hannah flagged one of the medical staff over. Jiao Ming glanced over and made eye contact with Zoe.

Jiao Ming whispered something to Hannah, who looked over at Zoe and nodded. Jiao Ming strode over to Zoe's cot, and Zoe attempted to prop herself up on her elbows. She fell back onto the pillows behind her. "Is Shane ok? What happened?"

"Shane . . . Powers just . . ." Jiao Ming took a long, shaky breath. Tears flowed freely from her puffy eyes. She sat in the chair beside Zoe's bed and said, "Morgan's dead."

Zoe blinked twice. "No. No, she can't be. We're so close."

Jiao Ming gripped the edge of the bed, trying to steady her shaking hands. "P-Powers just hanged her on national news. We all watched it happen."

Zoe let her own tears run down her cheeks. Loss surrounded her, suffocated her. "Fuck."

"I know." Jiao Ming took Zoe's hand in hers. "It was awful, Zo." Behind her, Shane had his head on Hannah's shoulder, sobbing into her T-shirt.

"We have to move," Zoe heard herself say. "We have to stop them from hurting anyone else."

"But you can't—"

"So someone will carry me or put me in a fucking

wheelbarrow. Leave me in a goddamned ditch somewhere. I don't care. Let's end this."

"Ok," Jiao Ming said. "Ok." She gripped Zoe's hand tighter, a gesture that supported both of them.

Isla slipped into the tent and headed straight for Zoe and Jiao Ming. "Are they doing anything for Shane?"

"Hannah was talking to them about something to sleep."

"Good." She ran a hand through her hair, staring off at a point past Zoe.

Zoe frowned. "It isn't your fault, Isla."

"Yeah."

"Morgan won't . . . she wouldn't want you thinking that way," Zoe said. She choked a bit on the bitter taste of the past tense. "We have to be stronger for her now."

Isla started crying again, tears coursing down her cheeks. "What if this was all for nothing?" Isla asked. "What if we lost her for nothing?"

"It's not for nothing," Zoe said, her voice rising. "Even if we lose. We're changing people's minds. That has to be something."

"But—"

"I might not walk again," Zoe said. "It sucks. But it's not for nothing. None of this is for nothing."

Jiao Ming put an arm around Isla, who rested her head on Jiao Ming's shoulder and pressed her lips together in an effort to suppress more tears. She shot a look at Zoe, who closed her own eyes. Isla wasn't who she was angry at.

Behind them, Shane howled.

Chapter Twenty Five

Jackson stormed into Powers' office, where Powers was consulting with two Militum captains. Powers had foregone the Oval Office for a more secluded room in the back, one without windows, after the third assassination attempt. He looked up as Jackson reached his desk. "Shore, what is this?"

Jackson slammed the newspaper he was holding onto Powers' desk. "Young's stunt is all over the news," he said. "They're not casting her execution as a warning. They're asking why they should fight for a president who's, in her words, 'letting the country burn.'"

"One think piece in a far-left paper is hardly all over the news," Powers said, peering at the front page. A photo of himself and Morgan dominated the cover. But it wasn't a far-left paper. It was one of Powers' own.

"The hashtags Let Him Burn and Fight for Morgan are trending on social media."

"It's illegal to—"

"People are wondering what the point was of killing a woman who was so visibly ill," Jackson interrupted. "Isla Logan somehow did an interview that's being picked up by major news shows across the country. They're all condemning her, but people are still seeing it."

"You have some nerve showing your face in here after your son ran off to join a bunch of domestic terrorists."

Shore recoiled as though slapped. "You've had a spy in our midst the whole time! Where is Ilana Cruz now?"

"You're out of line," Powers growled. "Go home for the rest of the day."

Jackson shot the president a look of pure venom before stomping out of the room, leaving the newspaper behind. He broke every speed limit on the way home and stormed into his house seething. He grabbed the framed photo that had been centered on the mantle of every home he'd occupied for the last twenty years: a picture of him, Madeline, and a young Christian, just a month before Madeline's death. He took that picture and chucked it against the wall, the glass shattering everywhere.

*   *   *

Christian huddled on his cot, his knees to his chest. No one wanted to share a tent with him, so he sat alone in the smallest one, catching his trembling breaths and attempting to steady his roiling stomach. *What on earth just happened? What just—*

The tent flap opened and Presley came in. She sat at the edge of Christian's bed. "We're going to need you now," she said.

"What?"

"You came here to join the revolution. We need you now more than ever."

Morgan's death flashed through his mind again: Powers leading her up to the platform, and then . . . "I don't know if I can do this," Christian admitted. "I don't know if I can fight."

"There isn't a neutral," Presley said. "You have to pick a side."

She got up to leave, stopped only momentarily by Christian's voice. "You," Christian said. "I choose you."

Presley stood for a moment, her hand on the tent's frame. Finally she said, "Good," and left Christian alone again.

Over the next week or so, Christian saw nothing of Shane, who walked alone behind the rest of the group according to Jiao Ming. She had offered to stay with him, as did Hannah and Isla. He didn't accept any of their offers.

So Christian did what he could with the other members of the group. He taught some of the newer members how to hold and handle a gun, just in case. He was a sharpshooter, like Morgan. He aided Isla in planning for a rally close to the capital. And he even agreed to do an interview with Parker.

While the rest of the group stopped, Christian, Parker, and Isla walked another half a mile up the trail. They had to stick largely to the real roads to travel rather than the trails since their group had gotten so big, but they still slept under the cover of the trees.

Parker had his camera ready to go. "Are you sure you want to do this?" Isla asked Christian.

"I know I don't want to," Christian answered. "I have to."

Isla stepped back, allowing Parker to set up the camera. He pointed it at Christian, and the green light came on. "Can you tell me who you are?"

Christian took a breath. "My name is Christian Shore," he said. "I'm the son of Jackson Shore, the vice president of the United States, and Madeline Shore. I'm an ex-Militum sergeant, and I'm fighting for the revolution because it's the right thing to do."

Parker nodded and asked, "How does it feel to speak out against your father?"

"I . . . I don't want to hurt my father. I do love him. But he's very misguided, and I can't let him hurt the people of this country just because he's my dad. The things he's done to people are things that no one should ever do. For years, I thought the Militum and the administration were in the right because of what I've been told: The rebels are all delusional and we are better than them. But now I know revolutionaries, and I've seen the things we've done to them in the name of protecting this country. We're not protecting this country. We're protecting ourselves, the people with power. It has to stop. And I want to help stop it."

"That's awesome, Chris," Parker said. "Anything else?"

Now or never. Part of him wanted it to be never. Still, Chris continued, "I'm adopted. I found out recently that my biological parents are revolutionaries. My father, he knew who they were, and he still pursued them. He killed one of them." Christian shook his head and looked back at Parker. "Can we stop?"

Parker shut the camera off. Christian looked back at Isla, who was now standing beside Shane.

Chris went to them both. "That was ok?"

"Really good," Isla said. "Thank you."

"You don't have to thank me." To Shane, he asked, "How are you?" Shane shrugged and Chris said, "Sorry, that was a stupid question."

Shane looked like he'd aged years in the last week. There were worry lines on his forehead and dark circles under his eyes. "It's ok," he said, his voice thick.

"I'm going to help Parker get the video up," Isla said. "Be careful out here, ok?"

"We will," Chris said. Isla left, and Shane sat on a wide stump sticking out of the ground. Chris sat beside him.

"You saw the end?"

"I saw it all," Shane said. "They're right. It was a great interview."

"Thanks." They sat in silence for another moment. "My father knew who Morgan was to me," Chris said finally. "And he killed her anyway." Chris wiped at his eyes. "I don't know why I thought he might not."

"I'm sorry," Shane said. "Like you said, he's misguided. He does love you."

"Yeah. Maybe."

"I can answer any questions you have," Shane said. "If . . . if you want."

Christian saw so much of himself in Shane now that he really looked. The way his face was shaped. The movements of his hands. Even the way Shane's shoulders slumped reminded Christian of himself when he'd lost his mother. "Yeah," he said. "I'd really like that." Christian hesitated before diving in, but Shane didn't rush him. "Um, did you ever have another child?"

Shane shook his head. "I didn't ever really need to be a parent, and Morgan was really against it. She . . . she was raped in the army and she just couldn't—" Shane closed his eyes. "I searched for her to get an abortion, but I couldn't find anyone who could do it safely. She said being forced to give birth was . . . almost as bad . . . ."

"Oh." Christian's stomach clenched painfully. After all that, they'd put her through so much more.

"It wasn't about you," Shane said. "I want you to know that."

"I do," he said. "What, um, what was she really like? Morgan? I only really ever got her yelling at me for being an asshole."

A ghost of a smile appeared on Shane's lips. "She was the best person I knew. Fearless. And funny. She just cared so much about everything. She wanted to make the world right, even though the world hadn't been right to her. She let me love her. It was the best thing anyone's ever done for me."

Part of Christian wished desperately that he had known her better. "Is there any other family?" he asked.

"No. Morgan's parents disowned her when she got pregnant and, well, wasn't married."

"They sound fucking delightful."

"My parents died some years ago. I have a sister, but we're not close anymore, really."

"Do you, well, are you upset that I found you?"

"No," Shane said. "Not at all."

Chapter Twenty Six

Jiao Ming knew Zoe wasn't particularly fond of traveling in Jelani Dennen's truck with Jelani and the tents instead of marching with the others, even if Jelani was nice enough and his wife said she didn't mind walking. But Hannah was working on building something Zoe could actually move in.

In the meantime, Zoe and Jiao Ming enjoyed the evenings together. As long as they didn't go too far, Jiao Ming could carry her there and back. Tonight, they sat by a stream close to their camp, sitting side by side and looking up at the stars.

"That one's Ursa Major," Zoe said, nodding up at the sky. "It's a bear."

"Really?"

"Who knows? Hannah pointed the bears out to me when we were traveling to California, but they're probably not in the same spot. I don't know how the sky works."

Jiao Ming laughed. "Definitely not in the same spot, Zo."

"Oh well. They're still pretty." She rested her head on Jiao Ming's shoulder. "I do love you, you know."

"Um, Zo?"

Zoe straightened out and frowned. "What's up?"

Jiao Ming felt hot, then cold, like the air around her was shifting. Her stomach did a backflip and she swallowed. "I know we've only actually known each other for like a year. And that's not a lot of time, but . . . I, well, I do love you, and finding you after the bombs went off, I was really, really scared I was going to lose you." Jiao Ming cleared her throat, and Zoe gazed back at her with wide eyes. "Anyway." She reached into the pocket of her jacket and took out a small, black box.

Zoe made a noise that sounded half like a gasp and half like she was being strangled. "Where did you even get that?"

"The, um, there was a town we stopped by, and Shane went to help me look. It turns out they were supporters of the revolution so major discount." Jiao Ming cringed. Her face flushed crimson. "Forget I said that."

"Jiao, I can't."

A beat. "You can't?"

"I mean, it just wouldn't be fair to you. I'm so broken." Zoe wiped at her tears.

"No. No. Stop it."

"It's true. I'm such a mess. I will literally never walk again. What kind of life—"

"Our life," Jiao Ming said. "It would be our life. I don't want to be with anybody else."

Zoe tried to hold a sob back and failed. "You mean it?"

"Of course I do. Do you want to marry me?"

"Yes. I do. I want to."

Jiao Ming kissed her, and Zoe raised her hands, embracing Jiao Ming's face, kissing her back fiercely. Jiao Ming wanted to freeze that moment forever, to live in Zoe's love and bury herself in their promises to each other. She was hardly even aware of slipping the ring on Zoe's finger, so delirious was she at the thought of their future.

It had been so long since any of them had heard such laughter that it took them a moment to identify the sound. Isla, Taylor, and Parker went to investigate and found Jiao Ming and Zoe, sitting by the running water, their foreheads pressed together. From the other side, Shane and Christian appeared at the edge of the river.

"What's going on?" Shane asked.

Zoe flashed her left hand at Shane. "I believe you had something to do with this?"

Taylor shrieked. "Holy shit."

Isla ran to them. "Let me see?" Zoe held out her hand, and Isla studied the ring: Small diamond studs circled the band. "Jiao Ming, this is stunning."

"Well, she got a discount," Zoe said, nudging Jiao Ming's ribs. Jiao Ming flushed, but she was still smiling.

"I don't know if you were planning on getting married, er, now," Parker said, "but it might be really great footage. Not that I—"

"Yes," Zoe said. "Absolutely."

"Do we have a priest or something?" Jiao Ming asked.

"I think we have a rabbi," Taylor said.

Zoe laughed. "That's fine with me if it's fine with Jiao." For the first time in weeks, Isla saw Zoe smile. For the first time in weeks, it felt like maybe they had a chance at being happy.

It took three days to get everything together for a wedding. They did, in fact, have a rabbi in their midst, Janet Dryfuss, and she was more than willing to do her part. From local allies, they found two dresses, and Hannah managed to finish Zoe's wheelchair in time for the ceremony.

"It's a good thing you're a genius," Zoe told her, playing with the brakes. "I was literally a mechanic, and I would have no idea how to do any of this." Hannah beamed.

They set up camp early that night, next to a clearing where Zoe would have enough space to move around. Parker found them two rings, and Presley and Taylor spent the day collecting flowers as they walked. As deep into fall as they were, flowers were few and far between, but they managed to find enough, and the weather stayed fair. When Parker asked if they wanted to get ready separately to avoid seeing each other before the ceremony, Zoe laughed and said, "I think it's a little bit late for tradition."

They came down the makeshift aisle together, both beaming. Everyone else wore their sweaters and jeans and whatever they happened to have with them, and they stood in loose rows. Shane, standing with Isla and Hannah in front, appeared genuinely happy for the first time since Morgan's death.

Jiao Ming sat at a stump by the rabbi, level with Zoe. Rabbi Dryfuss addressed the crowd. "Family and friends, welcome. With all the sorrow and all the pain in the world right now it brings me great joy to unite these two women, Jiao Ming See and Zoe Ivanova, in marriage. May their love remind us that there is still good and hope, and that by coming together, we may create a better world."

To Zoe and Jiao Ming, she said, "I believe you'd each like to say a few words?"

Jiao Ming took Zoe's hands. "Zoe," she said. "You are the bravest, most incredible person I've ever met. When I think about it, I really can't believe I'm lucky enough to be the person you want to spend your life with. I promise to love you forever, and to try to be as passionate and loving and fearless as you are. You're my everything."

Zoe just stared at her, wide-eyed and unable to stop smiling. "Fuck," Zoe mumbled, freeing one of her hands to wipe her eyes. "I have to follow that?" Jiao Ming laughed and Zoe took her hand again. "Jiao, you asked me when you proposed if I wanted to marry you, and I can't imagine a world in which the answer is no. You give me hope. That's everything I could have ever hoped for in a partner. I love you so much."

Dryfuss gestured for Isla to come forward. "You have the rings?"

Isla held them out to Jiao Ming and Zoe. They each took the other's. "Repeat after me, Zoe. I give you this ring. Wear it with love and joy. As this ring has no end, neither will my love for you."

Zoe smiled and blushed, suddenly shy. "I give you this ring. Wear it with love and joy. As this ring has no end, neither will my love for you." She slipped it onto Jiao Ming's finger, where it sparkled in the light of the sunset.

"Now Jiao Ming, repeat after me. With this ring, I marry you. As this ring has no end, neither will my love for you."

"With this ring, I marry you. As this ring has no end, neither will my love for you." Jiao Ming slipped the ring onto Zoe's finger, now crying.

"Well, that's it," Rabbi Dryfuss said. "Go ahead and kiss the bride."

Jiao Ming put her hands on the sides of Zoe's face and kissed her fiercely. Zoe's hands rose to Jiao Ming's, covering Jiao Ming's ring. They hardly heard their friends cheering, but they were, and loudly.

* * *

As their comrades mingled in the clearing, Shane took up residence on Jiao Ming's stump and watched her twirl Taylor under her arm to no music. The rest of the group distributed cheap beer among them.

Isla crouched beside him. "You ok?"

Shane jumped, just realizing he had company. "Yeah," he said, "I'm ok."

"It's ok if you're not, you know. I think Jiao Ming and Zoe would understand."

"When did you get to be so wise?" Shane asked. Partly in jest, partly not.

Isla shrugged. "Maybe after I was arrested by the Militum. Who's to say?"

Shane made a noise that might have been a laugh or a groan. He wasn't entirely sure what he intended anyway. Then he said, "It just feels strange. To be happy without her."

"I can't even imagine."

"She would have loved this," he said. "For Zoe and Jiao Ming, but it's also such a fuck you to the regime."

Isla looked over at Parker laughing with Jelani and his wife, at Hannah now weaving a flower crown for Zoe. "Our whole existence is kind of a fuck you to the powers that be, right?"

"Yes. You're right."

"I'll leave you alone now," she said. "Just wanted to let you know I'm here."

Shane offered her a small smile. "Thanks, Isla. It means a lot." He watched her retreat into the crowd, thinking that all of his happiest moments over the last twenty-five or so years were because of Morgan, about Morgan. He didn't want to let go of that. Not yet.

But he also knew Morgan would be furious if she knew any of this.

With a sigh, he moved to follow Isla, but was quickly stopped by Hannah, who had made him a flower crown of his own. He gave her a sideways grin and a small bow. "Thank you."

"Could we have everyone's attention please?"

Shane and Hannah both turned. Jiao Ming was standing on her stump now, her hands cupped around her mouth to make a megaphone. Zoe sat beside her, waiting. The din died down, and Jiao Ming said, "Thank you everyone for celebrating with us today. I just want to acknowledge the people that aren't here, because they've been taken or killed. Especially Morgan, who I know would be so happy to be here." She cleared her throat and reached for Zoe's hand. She raised her glass. "To Morgan."

"To Morgan," everyone else murmured, some of them taking their own drinks. Many of them knew her from her years transporting refugees. Many of them didn't. But they knew she had sacrificed her life for all of theirs.

They drank, and then Jiao Ming and Zoe made their way back to Shane and Hannah. "Was that ok?" Jiao Ming asked him.

Shane seemed to have forgotten how to form words. Instead, he pulled her into a tight hug, hoping to express everything he couldn't seem to verbalize. Jiao Ming pulled away and squeezed his arm, seeming to understand. Everything would have a shadow over it now. If not forever, then for a very long time.

* * *

Jackson Shore watched the wedding video with disdain. Not only were they getting an incredible amount of views on this stupid website no one seemed to be able to shut down, but they were practically spitting in the face of the administration by having two women get married.

As the women kissed on screen, he flipped to another tab where the video of his son was paused. He'd played it back so many times he could recite it verbatim, but he pressed play regardless.

"I—I don't want to hurt my father. I do love him. But he's very misguided, and I can't let him hurt the people of this country just because he's my dad. The things he's done to people are things that no one should ever do."

As Christian spoke, the video played images of Morgan Young on the stage before her execution. Would people make the connection between Morgan and his son, especially since Christian had mentioned that his biological parents were rebels? He hoped the camera at the execution had been far enough away to blur any similarities she bore to Christian, but he couldn't be sure.

"For years, I thought the Militum and the administration were in the right because of what I've been told, that the rebels are all delusional and we are better than them. But now I know revolutionaries, and I've seen the things we've done to them in the name of protecting this country. We're not protecting this country. We're protecting ourselves and our power. It has to stop. And I want to help stop it."

Jackson slammed the computer shut. The first time he heard those words— "I don't want to hurt my father. I do love him" —he cried. As much as Chris hurt him and as much as he had clearly hurt Chris, he did love him. So much. But love had to be secondary now.

Now, they were at war.

Chapter Twenty Seven

Isla stared out at where the crowd would stand with a knot in her chest. In the past few weeks, they had amassed nearly 200 travelers. More folks from nearby towns and from cities further away were planning to join them for their protest. News spread by word of mouth, since they didn't want Powers to catch wind of it ahead of time. There were always more bombs.

As Isla stood on the stage in the middle of a park not so far from their goal, she swallowed hard. A year ago, Isla would have laughed at anyone who told her she would be leading hundreds in protest. Now, it was just another day.

"Hey." Hannah came up at her shoulder. "You ok?"

"Yeah. Just nervous."

"You'll do great," Hannah said. "You've gotten really good at these things."

"I can talk to Parker on camera and lead meetings of a dozen people. This is a little bigger."

"The camera interviews are huge! You're reaching so many people."

"Parker can edit it first, though. He makes me sound good."

Hannah rolled her eyes. "Whatever. Zoe wanted to talk to you." Isla followed Hannah down the stairs and around to the side of the stage where Zoe stood with Parker. When they saw Isla approaching, Zoe said, "You still want me to speak, right?"

"Of course, yes."

"How?"

"What?"

Zoe gestured to her legs. "How am I supposed to get on the stage?"

Isla looked between Zoe and the stairs she and Hannah just descended. "Oh. Could we, I mean, if we put a ramp off the back, would that work?"

Zoe frowned. "Probably? This is all really new to me, too."

"We can work on that," Hannah said. "We still have a while."

"I'll help," Parker said. "Actually, I was talking to a new guy in our group who's a carpenter. Let's go find him." He and Hannah left, and Isla was left with Zoe.

"I am sorry," Isla said. "I didn't think—"

"Really, it's fine."

"It's not—"

"But you don't need to feel guilty about it. Learn from it and move on. You're doing fine." Zoe unlatched the brakes and rolled back a bit. "This is going to be good, ok? We're going to win."

"Yeah." Isla watched her leave, telling herself that what Zoe had said was true. There had to be hope, right? Otherwise, what was all of this for?

It was like the world had stopped. Isla tapped the microphone to check if it was on, and every single eye in the crowd turned to look at her, every person waiting for her to speak.

"Um. Hello." The microphone squealed with feedback, and Isla stepped back, covering her ears. In the front row, Hannah mouthed three words: You got this.

Just tell them the truth. That's all they want. They've been lied to for too long.

She grabbed the mic again and said, "I'm not great at the whole public speaking thing. I never thought I'd have to do anything like this, honestly, until the Militum arrested me for supposedly being a part of the revolution. I wasn't then. But because of their actions, I am now." There was scattered applause, a whistle or two.

"A lot of you know who I am because of the videos our expert technician Parker has put up on our website," she continued, sending Parker a brief smile in the audience, where he was filming her every move. "Today you're going to hear from some of us about what the Militum has done to us and our families. We have people ready to talk and expose the regime for what it really is. And then tonight, we march." More applause, louder this time and from everywhere, swollen with the crowd's readiness for this moment.

Isla stood behind the stage with Shane, Zoe, and Jiao Ming as Taylor took the stage. They spoke about their mom and their time living as a volunteer in refugee housing. Then Parker stepped up, entrusting his camera to Hannah, to talk about becoming a refugee and what it was like to be able to share everyone else's stories. Faiza talked about her time as a guide, and then Rabbi Dryfuss spoke of her congregation's fears and experiences: Several teens had come out to her in tears, and every once in a while, someone she knew had disappeared without a trace. As she stepped away, Presley took the stage.

Presley began by looking out over the crowd, but not like Isla had. Presley exuded confidence. Isla thought she could never do that, until Shane said, "I'm so impressed with all of you."

"What?"

"You all look like you own the stage. Like it's your turn to talk and the crowd is going to listen."

"All of us?"

"She'll never believe you," Zoe said. "Isla doesn't realize how much people listen to what she has to say." Isla flushed and turned back to the stage, where Presley stood, speaking to the crowd. "I left the States for California two years ago, when I was eighteen. I left because that year someone I trusted raped me and I got pregnant. I have a medical thing that makes giving birth really dangerous for me and the baby, so I found a place that would do an abortion. It wasn't safe. I got really sick after, actually, but my mom took care of me. I think she knew, but she never said."

Isla's stomach dropped. In all the months they'd known each other, she never thought to ask Presley why she was in California. "I don't know how they found out, but one day, Militum guys showed up at our door and asked about someone having an abortion," Presley continued. "They wouldn't believe it when we said no one did, so my mom told them it was her. She's pretty young, so they b-believed her." Presley wiped her eyes and took a breath. "They believed her. They took her away while I was screaming. She d-died in prison. And the next day, I ran."

Presley swallowed and clutched the mic. "I didn't say

anything when she was taken away, so I'm saying something now. This can't keep going on. My mom mattered. We matter. So let's show them that they can't ignore us anymore." Presley exited the stage to incredible applause. Christian, who was coming on, gripped her shoulder. "I'm sorry," he said quietly. "You didn't deserve any of that."

Presley nodded and walked off. At the center of the stage, Christian grabbed the mic. He froze, and people began to whisper. Isla thought she knew why. Nearly everyone there, after all, had watched his interview.

"I'm Chris," he began. "Chris Shore. Until a short while ago, I was a Militum sergeant." The whispers grew louder, and Christian looked back at them. At Shane. Still facing away from the crowd but close enough to the microphone, he said, "I've done some terrible things as a Militum sergeant and officer, and I've seen worse. But let me just say that the system they've set up isn't broken. It's working exactly as it was designed to. And that's why we have to overhaul it." The whispers became murmurs, with a smattering of applause.

He went on to describe the lies they tell Militum recruits, the lies he bought his whole life. He detailed for them Adam Boeck's murder, the treatment of Morgan in captivity. "We let her lie dying on a dirty floor for months," Christian said. "And still, the moment I went to her and asked her to give me a chance, she did. I'd never experienced that kind of openness before. And we killed her in front of the entire country."

A breath, and then he continued, "I know a lot of you watched my interview where I talked about having biological parents in the revolution. I learned just before she was killed that Morgan Young was my biological mother. My father killed her anyway." The whispers in the crowd picked up again, making Isla flinch. She knew Christian and Shane had discussed this ahead of time, but it still must be terrifying. Beside her, Shane watched, frozen.

"I don't want to talk about these things," Christian said. "They're horrifying and painful. But you need to know what we're up against. These people don't care about you, and I know that because I was one of them. So we are going to get rid of the Militum. And we're going to replace them with a system that works just as well. But for us, not them."

Christian's applause was the loudest yet. No one seemed more surprised than Christian himself, who stood at the mic, stunned, before he remembered how to move. He passed Zoe and Jiao Ming coming up onto the stage and the applause grew thunderous. As Parker told them repeatedly, the response to the wedding video had nearly overwhelmed their servers.

The applause continued as Jiao Ming adjusted the mic and kissed Zoe quickly on the cheek, meaning to move offstage. Instead, Zoe grabbed her hand and pulled her into a real kiss, a longer kiss, and the noise turned from thunderous to deafening.

Jiao Ming finally walked back to Isla and Shane, blushing fiercely. Zoe took the mic and said, "Clap all you want, as long as you know she's taken." Laughter from the crowd, and Zoe smiled in acknowledgement. "For real, though, after so many years of hiding such a big part of who I am, it's incredible to stand on stage with the woman I love and have that be celebrated."

Behind the stage, as the crowd whooped their approval, Isla said, "She's incredible. They love her."

"She's relating to them," Shane said quietly.

Zoe reiterated much of what she'd spoken about with Parker in her own interviews. Aviva. Her being a guide for nearly a decade. "I don't know if you all watched the interviews on Parker's incredible website," she continued, "but I wasn't in a wheelchair when I gave those. But I was at my wedding." The audience descended into silence as Zoe recounted the bombing. She told them about finding the boy, Kyle, and about the shop exploding. "The thing was, when we got back to camp, only two of our tents had been hit, but the town had been decimated. They weren't aiming for us. They were using the civilians as bait, knowing we would go to help them. They hurt innocent people, destroyed their livelihoods and nearly killed them, so they could maintain power. Those aren't the kind of people I want in charge.

"I won't walk again. But that's not the worst part of remembering that day. It's remembering the terrified faces of those people we put in basements for an unknown amount of time. It's the weight of the little boy under me as we were attacked. I'm fighting for them, so that no one has to feel that kind of fear ever again."

Again, the crowd went absolutely crazy for Zoe, and Jiao Ming came back to help her off the stage. Shane took another breath beside Isla, but made no move to go. Isla put a hand on his arm. "Are you sure you want to do this?"

"No," he said. And then he went anyway.

There were no murmurs as Shane got up onto the stage, no applause. He had never done an interview with Parker before. Most of the folks in the audience didn't know who he was. He spotted Hannah toward the front, smiling up at him, and he spoke directly to her: "Thank you all for coming out today." Hannah nodded, and he said, "My name is Shane Wilson. I was a refugee living in California. And for twenty years I was married to Morgan Young."

The murmurs began then, but they weren't unsure or

judgmental. They were empathetic. Shane put a hand on the mic to steady it and kept his eyes on Hannah and Parker. He could tell this to them. "I haven't done an interview yet. I've made excuse after excuse, but really, it was too painful for me. But it would be dishonoring Morgan not to talk about her here. She was so incredible. For years, she brought people who feared for their lives to the border. She fought in the war until she was shot and sent home to recover, and then she continued to fight long after the rest of us had given up. This is the woman that President Powers k-killed. Sh-she w-was—" Shane took a step back from the mic and took a few gasping breaths. He could do this. He had to.

He stepped forward again. "The reason Morgan can't speak to you all today is because Powers killed her to send a message to the rest of us. So we're going to send him a message. That he can't scare us into submission. We have everything to lose. Believe me. But we have so much more to gain if we succeed. We have to do it for each other and with each other. We have to do it because no one else will do it for us." Shane stepped back again for a moment, then left without really finishing, unable to say anymore. Isla gave him a small smile as she passed him on the stage. As Isla addressed the crowd for a final time, she looked behind her and saw Shane; his head was on Jiao Ming's shoulder, and her arms were wrapped around him, letting him cry onto her shoulder.

Chapter Twenty Eight

It was hot in the crowd of several hundred, but Hannah tried not to let it bother her. She stayed close to Isla as they marched down the streets, chanting and holding signs that said "What will you die for, Mr. President?" and "No Justice, No Peace."

Just behind Hannah, Isla, and Taylor, Christian kept close to Shane. "This is your first protest?" Shane asked. Christian nodded, and Shane said, "Mine too."

Hannah turned and frowned. "Really?"

Shane gave her a small smile. "Morgan always tried to get me to go. I don't think I saw the point. We had already lost the war. But she was always smarter than I was."

Christian put a hand on Shane's arm. "Well, I'm glad you're here now."

"Yeah. Me too."

Together, their caravan traversed the streets, finally in the same state as the regime they aimed to overthrow.

They saw the barricade as they rounded the corner: Militum officers, each holding a black baton. Their holsters held their guns and canisters of mace. Hannah's heart flipped into her mouth as they neared, and she nearly stopped breathing. She was only vaguely aware when Zoe cut out in front of them and went straight up to a man in a captain's uniform. "Is there a problem, sir?"

Zoe had insisted on being the one to confront the Militum should there be any. When Shane reminded her that they would have no problem assaulting a woman just because she was in a wheelchair, she said to make sure Parker had his camera rolling then. And Parker did: The camera on his phone was broadcasting the whole thing live to their website. The captain glanced over at Parker before turning back to Zoe. "Do you have a permit for this, er, event, ma'am?"

"We're marching peacefully."

"It's illegal to protest without a permit." Which basically just meant it was illegal to protest.

"A good friend of mine once said that just because something is illegal doesn't mean it's wrong." Beside Hannah, Isla stifled a grin.

"We're going to ask you once to leave," the captain said. "And then we're going to make you."

Her heart was pounding, but Zoe only raised an eyebrow. "No."

Quick as a whip, the captain tugged his mace free and sprayed as much of it as he could into Zoe's face. Before she could even scream, the rest of the Militum officers reacted, charging at the protesters with chemicals and batons. That was when Hannah lost track of everything.

*   *   *

Jiao Ming pulled Zoe back and pushed her out of the line of fire onto the sidewalk, closely followed by Shane. Zoe bent over gagging and gasping for air when Shane handed her a jug of milk he'd grabbed from Faiza. "Zo, use this."

She grabbed it blindly, pouring it over her eyes and mouth. Jiao Ming's grip was viselike on Zoe's leg. "Milk?"

Shane gestured to himself. "Former army medic. I've been teargassed before."

Zoe began coughing, and Jiao Ming turned back to her. "Zoe?"

"I'm ok," she choked out. Her eyes were bright red and streaming. "Isla and Hannah—"

"You go," Shane said, taking the rest of the milk back. "I'll make sure they're ok."

"But—"

"Go."

Still shaking and half blind from the mace, Zoe let Jiao Ming take her somewhere safe. Shane scanned the crowd, trying to figure out where the girls could have gone.

* * *

Hannah knew where they were supposed to meet up, but she didn't want to go without Isla, whom she'd lost after the Militum began spraying what she thought might be massive amounts of teargas with huge hoses. Hannah fell to the side of the street, hacking and crying. Like Zoe, she was covered in milk, her eyes bloodshot. Then, from behind her, a scream.

Hannah whipped around. Christian was on his knees in front of her. An officer stood over him with a baton held high, ready to strike again, when one of the other protesters fell over him. The officer was distracted enough that Hannah was able to yank Christian up by the back of his shirt and push him to the back of the mass of bodies, where he fell against a pole clutching his arm. "I think it's broken," he hissed.

"What just happened?" Hannah asked.

"That officer was aiming at you, and I didn't think you saw so I moved—"

"Let's get you out of here." She took hold of Christian's arm, the one that hadn't taken a beating, and wove through the crowd. More Militum were moving in by the minute. She stepped over another body, one she wasn't sure was still alive. But she had one mission, and she didn't stop to check.

She led Christian back to the makeshift camp that had been set up by volunteers during the march. They went straight to the medical tent, where several people were already being treated for teargas burns and broken bones. But she didn't see Isla or Shane or Presley or—

"Hannah?" Jiao Ming was in front of her now. "Are you ok?"

"Have you seen Isla?"

"No. Not since the barricade."

"Do you . . . do you think—"

"She'll be ok, Hannah. She will."

Hannah tried to keep herself from shaking. "Can I help?"

"Only if you're sure you're ok." Hannah nodded again and followed Jiao Ming back to the patients.

It was another hour before Isla, Taylor, and Shane came back, all bruised and exhausted but very much alive. Hannah was talking to Presley, who had skinned her palms and knees in a bad fall but was otherwise ok, when they came into the tent. Hannah jumped up and ran to Isla, throwing her arms around her sister's neck. "You're ok!"

"Oh, fuck, Hannah." Isla held her just as tightly. For the first time all day, Hannah's heart slowed to a normal speed.

When they finally let go, Hannah went to hug Shane, and Isla went over to Jiao Ming and Zoe. "Faiza was arrested," she said. "Maybe fifty of us total and more of the civilians. And two dead."

Zoe exhaled and her shoulders slumped. "Who?" she asked.

"Sean McGaffrey. I didn't know him, but he was fifteen years old and had an asthma attack when they sprayed the teargas. And Rabbi Dryfuss."

Zoe moaned and appeared to deflate further into herself. Jiao Ming covered her eyes with one hand and took Zoe's with the other. Zoe regained composure first and asked, "Parker? I haven't seen him."

"He's ok. Shaken, but ok. Kevin was with him when I saw them last. I think everyone with serious injuries is here." Two beds down, Jelani Dennen lay whimpering on his side, still blinded by the teargas after an hour. Beside him, a medic was probing at Christian's arm, which Christian couldn't let go of without feeling excruciating pain.

"Ok," Zoe said. "Ok."

"You were amazing, by the way," Isla told her. "Talking to the Militum captain. I couldn't have been that calm."

"Yes you could have," Zoe insisted. Beside them, Hannah took up residence on an empty bed with Shane, and Taylor took Isla's hand.

To Zoe, Isla said, "No. You're really amazing, the way you talk to them. And you were amazing at the rally."

"Oh yeah," Hannah added. "Better than any Powers' speech I've seen."

Zoe rolled her eyes. "That's not a high bar."

"I'd vote for you for president," Taylor offered.

"Mmhmm, yeah, I'm sure the rest of the country would be down to vote for a lesbian in a wheelchair."

Jiao Ming frowned. "Zoe—"

"I'm tired," Zoe interrupted, suddenly sobered. She squeezed Jiao Ming's hand. "Can we go?"

"Oh. Yeah. Sure." They left, and Shane stood. "I'm going to see if they need any help," he said, and then he, too, was gone. Before Hannah left to say goodnight to Presley and check up on Christian, she watched Isla leave the tent, sliding her hand into Taylor's, grasping at the connection. She was happy for them both. But she also felt a kind of loss.

Chapter Twenty Nine

Dexter Powers couldn't tear his eyes from the hoard of people congregated around the White House. Signs said "Powers Resign!" and "Hang the President Instead!" and "What will you die for, Mr. President?" He knew the rebels would soon be at his gates. Several of them had weapons, and at least two Militum men stationed at the capitol's borders were dead, though so were several rebels. They were now threatening to remove Powers by force. There was no option to come quietly.

A knock on the door, and then a Militum captain was in his office. "We don't have the manpower to keep driving them back, Mr. President," he said. "What should we do now?"

Powers sighed. They had been pepper spraying and shooting rubber bullets at the protesters for days now, arresting known local activists, and more. But the protesters kept coming back, and in bigger numbers. Powers' wife and daughters had been moved to a safe house. "Keep doing what you're doing," he said. "We'll have to change tactics when the rebels arrive, but . . ." he trailed off, and the captain seemed to understand.

"Of course, Sir."

"Actually. All Militum officers should retreat."

"Sir?"

"Stay at the prison. Await my instruction."

"Yes, Sir." The captain left, shutting the door behind him. After the video of one of his captains macing the Ivanova woman went live, public opinion turned from bad to worse. Protesters were shouting for his resignation and many of them for his death.

The rebels wanted him dead. That was exactly what they would get.

* * *

At last, they reached the president. And it was terrifying.

The afternoon after the protest, Isla found herself leading a march to the White House, protesters lining the street and applauding the revolutionaries coming up the road. Many of them were young, Isla or Hannah's ages, and several of them wore Children of the Revolution T-shirts. Several of them cheered for Isla specifically. She wasn't entirely sure how she felt about that.

Taylor came up behind her. "You're doing great," they said. "We're almost there."

Almost there.

The door burst open under the combined strength of Shane and Parker. Isla led the others in. To their surprise, there were no Militum officers waiting, no defenses at all. Isla frowned and made her way up the stairs, followed by Shane and Jiao Ming. Gun forward, she made her way through the maze of winding halls, recalling the map Parker had helped her memorize. At last, she arrived at the president's office and kicked the door in.

Powers sat behind his desk, his hands on the dark wood. It

was the first time Isla had seen the man in person. He looked more drawn than she would have thought. Smaller.

"Isla Logan, I presume." Powers rose, ignoring the three guns pointed at his head. "I saw your interviews."

"You're going to need to come with us," Isla said, sounding a lot calmer than she felt. What motivation did he have to do so other than his life? She knew he had two daughters and prayed that the hope of seeing them again would be enough.

"Oh, I have no intention of doing that," Powers said. "Ms. Logan, have you ever killed anyone before?"

"Isla ignore him," Shane called. To Powers he said, "C'mon."

"Because by the time you leave this office," Powers said, "I'm afraid you might be a murderer."

"No," she said, shaking her head. "Even if I kill you, that doesn't make me a murderer."

"Oh really?"

Isla swallowed. What was he playing at? "It's justified," she said.

"Is it?" Powers asked. "What if I were unarmed, Ms. Logan?"

"I'm not going to kill you then."

"Really? Then why, may I ask, do you have a weapon when I have none?"

"You're coming with us," Shane said, tucking his gun in his belt and walking around Isla.

Everything happened so fast after that. Powers pulled his own gun out of his belt and aimed it at Shane. Isla took aim and fired at Powers.

Behind her, Jiao Ming screamed. The former president of the United States staggered back against the wall, blood blooming from his chest, and sank to the floor. Isla heard the same buzzing in her head as when she'd watched Morgan die, and she blinked herself back into focus.

"Heh," Powers made a noise somewhere between a laugh and a cough. Blood leaked from the corner of his lips. "Unarmed," he mumbled. And then his eyes rolled back in his head.

Isla set her gun on the ground and ran a hand over her face. Her heart pounded, and her head spun. "I did it," she whispered. "I killed him."

"No, Isla." Shane went to her as Jiao Ming ran past them. He put his hands on Isla's shoulders. "He would have killed me. You didn't—"

"It was empty."

"What?" Shane and Isla both turned to Jiao Ming, who had Powers' gun in her hands.

"No bullets," she said. "It was empty." She showed them the gun. There were no bullets in the chamber.

Isla just stared for a moment. "It's over," she said. "Powers surrendered." She leaned back against the wall and let herself sob.

The three of them left the president's office together and ran straight into Hannah and Taylor coming up the stairs, guns drawn.

"He wasn't there?" Taylor asked.

"He's dead," Isla said, her voice hoarse. "Powers is dead."

Hannah blanched. "How?"

"He's in the office. I . . . I shot him." Bile rose in Isla's throat, and she forced it back down. But she couldn't get rid of the image. Is that what her parents looked like, after? Did this make her a murderer, like Powers said?

"It's done," she said. "We won."

And, yet, it still wasn't over.

* * *

Jackson Shore was wasted. He had been wasted for several hours, ever since he'd heard the rebels would be at his gates, and he was wasted when they burst through his door, guns in front, led by his son.

"Relax," he said, holding up his half-empty scotch glass. "I'm unarmed."

Christian pointed his gun with his right hand. His left arm was in a sling. "Put down the glass, Dad."

He did just that, setting it on a coaster the texture of a cork board. "So. You're here. Take me away, then."

Another rebel holstered their gun and came toward Jackson with handcuffs. The whole time, Jackson kept his eyes on Christian. "I was going to burn your adoption papers, you know. I almost had, and then I chickened out last minute. If I had, would you have joined the rebels?"

"Revolutionaries," Christian corrected.

"Would you?"

Christian's eyes narrowed. "I don't know."

"Hmm." Christian didn't know why Jackson asked. He wouldn't have felt better either way. "Is this what you wanted, my son?"

Christian shook his head. "No. But you have to be stopped."

"You know, I didn't know if I wanted children. Not until

your mother. Madeline made me want to love someone else. You were the best thing to ever happen to me." His face darkened then, and he said, "When she died, I couldn't stand not knowing who your biological parents were. What were the odds?"

In. Out. In. Out. Christian took several deep breaths, focusing only on exhaling as he held back tears. He couldn't start crying now, when they were so close to done. At last, Jackson said, "Fine, fine. Take me away then."

Christian locked eyes with Parker, who was holding Jackson's wrists tight, and said, "Take him." Parker led Jackson away, Jackson stumbling all the while. Christian waited until all the revolutionaries left. Then, he went exploring.

He hadn't grown up in this house, even as a child, Christian moved around a lot, mostly in line with Jackson's job, but he was familiar with it. He immediately noticed the photo missing from the mantle.

Frowning now, Christian circled the house, searching for it. Maybe it wasn't there at all, but he had to check. He wasn't sure why, but he did. Finally, he found the frame, shattered, behind the chair in the room he'd started his search in. Carefully, avoiding glass shards, Christian lifted the photo of him and his parents. That moment, captured by the camera, was perhaps the last time Christian could remember being happy.

Chapter Thirty

Although Powers had Morgan's body cremated, Ilana Cruz was still able to show Shane where her ashes would have been scattered. "She wasn't the first," Ilana said, disdain etched in the lines of her weary face. "But at least she'll be the last."

"That was all she wanted," Shane said. "No more senseless deaths." They stood on a rock overlooking the ocean. It was nearly dusk, and the sun's golds and reds reflected across the surface of the waves.

"I'll leave you," Ilana said. "Just don't stay too long, ok?"

Once Ilana left, Shane pulled out a letter from his pocket, one he'd written after receiving Morgan's and after witnessing her death.

Dear Morgan,

I could not say why I am writing this letter. It was Hannah's idea, something to do to express my grief over your loss. Morgan, watching you so bravely face the imminent prospect of your own death broke me. It left a chasm in my chest that I'm not sure I'll ever be able to fill. Part of me died with you that day.

You would be so proud of Hannah and Isla. They've both stepped up so much and taken on this revolution as their own. They care so deeply. They remind me of you in that way. Jiao Ming, too, has stepped up beyond what anyone could have expected of her, and Zoe is, as usual, brilliant in her activism. We all miss you more than I can put into words.

As you apologized for the brevity of your letter (of which you had no need to), I must apologize for the disjointed nature of mine. There is so much I want to say to you, even if you will never read these words. To that end, I want to thank you for writing to me. It's given me something to hold on to, a little bit of hope for the future, even though you are not here to see it. I have so many things I want to thank you for—most of them have to do with you just being you—but this is the most concrete and the most immediate.

Christian and I have connected briefly, though I have not spoken much to anyone these last few days. His eyes are so much like yours, Morgan, that it hurts to look at them, but I will try. He's lost, and I will help him try to find his direction. Not because he is biologically ours, but because he deserves this, as anyone does. I do think he has a good heart, even if he's done terrible things.

In your letter, you also noted the importance of continuing to make the world a better place without you. With our friends and allies, I will do my part to continue to fight, as much as I am tempted to give up. I wanted this better world for us, but I will have to make it better now for everyone else. Your death will not be for nothing. I promise you that.

I will always love you, Morgan. And I'm sorry we could not save you. Now, we'll have to work on saving our country.

All my love forever,

    Shane

He folded the paper into thirds and brought out a lighter he'd borrowed from Kevin on the condition that Shane didn't tell his parents, even though everyone knew that Kevin smoked. Shane lit the letter aflame and let the breeze take the ashes with it. As the last of his letter disappeared, Shane closed his eyes. *I'm sorry.*

Christian waited for Shane to come back up the path so they could walk back to camp together. Ilana was working on putting them all up in hotels, but neither Christian nor Shane felt any particular rush to get there. When Shane joined him, Christian asked, "Was it nice at least?"

"Beautiful." Shane looked over at Christian as they began walking, this man who was hardly a man but who looked so much like him, and whom he was just beginning to know. "You knew Powers, didn't you?"

"I did. He was slimy and weak, but I never wanted this. Do you think that makes me selfish?"

"No, of course not. I think that makes you human." Shane glanced back over his shoulder at the footprints they were leaving behind. "Next time, would you like to come with me? To see where Morgan's ashes were scattered?"

For a moment, Christian forgot how to breathe. "Yes," he said. "I would love that."

* * *

Taylor, a California native, opted out of attending the meeting, leaving Isla, Hannah, Zoe, Jiao Ming, Shane, Faiza, Presley, and Parker. Shane also invited Christian, but he declined, opting instead to visit his father in prison. Jiao Ming and Zoe came in last. Jiao Ming set a chair aside, so Zoe could maneuver her wheelchair closer to the table.

"How are you feeling?" Isla asked Zoe. It had been weeks since the bombings, and Zoe still got headaches every few days and migraines at least every other week. The mace attack at the protest hadn't helped, either.

"Better," she said, flipping the brakes. "Still getting headaches, but they're not so bad."

"Let's start, then," Isla said. "For now, Ilana has taken charge of making sure the country doesn't fall apart. But we need to put an actual system in place. A democracy."

"We had a democracy," Presley said. "It led to a dictatorship."

"Only because we allowed the president to have so much power," Faiza said. "We'd need to reconfigure checks and balances and all that. And replace the Militum with community systems in the meantime."

"Supreme Court," Zoe said. "This whole one man putting all his people in for life thing is not going to fly."

"Ok, so we propose term limits," Isla said, looking over their outline. That was on there already, but she supposed it didn't hurt to talk it out. "What else?"

"The Electoral College," Parker added. "I don't think the Founding Fathers ever intended it to work in a country this big. It's the only reason we got presidents like Powers in the first place."

"I don't see the point in any of this, honestly," Presley said from the other end of the table. "I mean, who's to say no one will try to take over again? There will always be someone who sees an opening to rise up by putting other people down. There will always be people willing to tear families apart."

Isla remembered Presley's speech, her rare display of emotion, and knew she must be hurting. Nothing they did now would bring Presley's mom back, or Isla and Hannah's parents. She opened her mouth to speak, but Zoe got there first. "You're right," she said. "Powers was that person. And we beat him."

"Powers isn't the only one," Presley argued.

"I know that. But there will always be people to rise up and fight back against a dictator. They never last." Presley shrugged, and Zoe continued, "Giving a shit gives you power, even though it hurts. I'm choosing to believe that."

Presley looked up into Zoe's eyes, and Zoe nodded. Finally, Presley said, "Gerrymandering. People shouldn't be able to reconfigure districts in order to get more votes. That's also a reason we ended up here."

That last one wasn't on their agenda. Beside Isla, Hannah took the outline from under her hands and scribbled it down.

"Hey." Taylor stepped away from the wall as Isla exited the building. She and Hannah were the last to leave.

Hannah looked over at Taylor, then at Isla. "I'll catch you later."

"Bye." Isla watched her sister walk away, then went to Taylor. "I actually need to talk to you."

"Sure."

Isla sat on the steps, motioning for Taylor to sit beside her. "Look, I really like you."

"Ah. This is a breakup."

"No. Yes. I'm sorry." Isla had contemplated for a while now what her future might look like. In no instance could she see herself working on a relationship with Taylor in the midst of the chaos that was her country.

"I get it. There's a lot going on right now, all that. I'm

upset, but I'm not mad. And I'm not surprised." They pressed their lips together and fell silent.

"I do really like you though," Isla insisted. "You're a good person, Taylor."

"Yeah. Maybe we can still be friends?"

Isla wasn't sure. She'd never broken up with someone before, much less her first crush, her first kiss, possibly her first love. Regardless, she said, "Sure. I'd like that."

"Cool. Well, um, that's it, then. I'm going to go cry in my tent now." Taylor stood. "You're really special, Isla. Never forget that."

They left without another word, and Isla watched them go, following Hannah's path. She didn't cry, but there was a heaviness in her chest, for Taylor and for everything else. She wasn't sure about Taylor, but she wasn't sure about much of anything right now. A year ago, she hadn't known what the Supreme Court was, and now she was helping rebuild the country.

But she had to try. That was all she could do.

Epilogue

Isla sat beside Hannah as the lecture hall filled. Zoe gave a talk at least once a year, but being the former president of the United States, her lectures were always packed. As usual, Hannah had saved Isla a seat in the front next to her. When Jiao Ming came, she would sit with them, but Jiao Ming was in court that day with a client, an immigrant from Colombia. Her and Zoe's son usually sat with his friends in the back, but he always stopped by to say hello. Come fall, their daughter would start school here.

"Thanks," Isla said, sliding into the not-so-comfortable auditorium chair. "How was lunch?"

"We only got stopped by two people for selfies," Hannah laughed. "You would have hated it."

"Too bad I had class," Isla said. "Selfies for you or Zoe?"

"Obviously Zoe. No one knows who I am, and I'd like to keep it that way."

That wasn't, strictly speaking, true. Along with her other compatriots, Isla mentioned Hannah by name in her books on the revolution. It was true, though, that Hannah managed to fly further under the radar than Zoe or Jiao Ming, or even Isla herself.

Occasionally, Isla would give a talk as a history professor, or Hannah as an astronomy professor. Isla usually had to work hard to understand a word of the latter. After all these years, space still confused her. Mostly, she came because she loved how Hannah shined when she spoke about the stars.

The buzz of the auditorium dimmed as Zoe and her assistant entered with two secret service agents, but quickly picked back up again as Zoe busied herself at the podium. She spotted Isla and Hannah and winked.

After, Isla and Hannah watched and waited as students went up to Zoe, shepherded by secret service agents, to ask her questions. What advice would she give? What about this policy? After nearly half an hour, Zoe's assistant ushered the students away, leaving Zoe with Isla and Hannah. One of the agents hovered in the background. "We missed you at lunch, Isla," Zoe said.

"Hannah told me you got stopped for photos," Isla said. "I'm not mad I missed it."

"Excuse me? President Ivanova?" Behind them, a young man with a Young University sweatshirt and square glasses fidgeted with his pen. "I, um, I'm a grad student here. Political science. I just want to say I really enjoyed your lecture."

"Thank you," Zoe said. The young man didn't move.

"I wanted to ask . . . were you part of the group of revolutionaries that cleared out Greensdale before the bombs went off? It would have been a little over twenty-two years ago? I mean, I know you were."

"Yes. I was." It was a painful memory for all of them, but yes, she was there. She almost died there.

"You, well, saved a boy that day. In a flower shop." The student took a breath. "That boy was me. I just wanted to thank you for saving my life."

Isla looked back at Zoe, who just stared. To the student, Isla said, "What's your name?"

"Kyle," he said. "Kyle Mohapatra."

"Well, Kyle, I think you might be the only person to ever make Zoe speechless."

"You're welcome, I guess," Zoe managed. "I have to go talk to a class in twenty minutes, but, um, I can give you my personal email maybe?"

"Yes. Absolutely."

"Great." Zoe smiled, and Kyle handed her his phone. Next to them, Hannah laughed. "Oh, Jiao Ming's going to be so mad she missed this."

*   *   *

Shane had been expecting the call, but still, seeing Hannah's name pop up on the screen made him smile. "Hello?"

"You'll never guess what happened today." She always did that. Never hello. Just launched right into the conversation.

"Really? What?"

Hannah explained what happened with Kyle Mohapatra, the stunned look on Zoe's face, how they were planning to stay in touch. Shane listened with interest, but part of his mind was elsewhere.

It was twenty-two years today that Morgan had been murdered by a regime she'd spent half her life trying to overthrow. And in those twenty-two years, he always heard from Hannah. Zoe and Jiao Ming would always call around the day, as would Christian, and he often heard from Isla, but Hannah was the only one who called every single year, on the exact anniversary. That first year, he was still living nearby, and she visited. They spoke about what happened, but Hannah, seeing how it brought Shane pain, began to tell him about school and about some stupid thing that happened over lunch. Shane didn't remember any more than that. He just remembered how much it had lifted his heart.

"Anyway," Hannah said. "How are you doing?"

"Hanging in there," he said, leaning back on his couch. "Planning to visit soon."

"Please do. The kids keep asking about you."

"I absolutely will."

"Are you missing her today?"

Shane clutched the phone tightly, painfully. "Every day," he admitted.

"She'd be really happy," Hannah said. "She would have been amazed by how far we've come."

Shane glanced out his window. There were children playing on the street, the neighborhood kids. Some of their parents or grandparents were former American refugees—California had rejoined the United States several years prior. But there were no new ones coming in, no need for refugee housing. The apartments Shane, Hannah, and the others had occupied when they first came to California were turned into housing for people experiencing homelessness.

"Yes," he said. "She would have."

*   *   *

Jaquan rarely left town for work, and it's not like Isla ever wanted him to. But when he did, she relished the chance to spend time with their three girls. Their two youngest had after-school activities on Wednesdays, so she and Leanne went to the park for an hour before heading over to the elementary school to pick them up. Leanne pointed to the Morgan Young Memorial Park sign with the hand that wasn't holding her ice cream cone. "You knew her, right? Our Morgan is named after her?" she asked, referring to Christian and Presley's daughter, one of two twins a year younger than Poppy.

"Yeah. She was my teacher."

"We started learning about the revolution today," Leanne said between licks. "Mrs. Robinson mentioned you."

"Oh yeah?"

"Mmhmm. A bunch of the other kids asked me about it, but I don't actually know that much."

Isla smoothed her daughter's hair out of her eyes. "Well, would you like to?"

"Sure."

"I don't really know where to start," Isla said. She'd spoken to her girls somewhat about her history, about her trauma, but this was the first time one of them actually asked about the revolution directly. She still sometimes woke up with nightmares about the bombing, about her parents' death, about Morgan's capture. She supposed she always would. They were fewer now, but they still happened, and Jaquan would wake up with her and calm her down. He made her feel safe. She supposed that was part of why she loved him.

"I guess I can start with where I started," she said. "I was eighteen when I left the States."

Leanne took a bite out of her cone and listened. Isla explained her journey—sleeping in the woods, making it to California—to her daughter. Soon, they had to leave to get Leanne's sisters, who would probably distract Leanne from

wanting to know more. But that was ok.
They would learn.

Acknowledgements

First and foremost, I want to thank my readers, without whom writers would just be shouting into a void. So thank you, thank you, THANK YOU, for thinking this story worthy of your time. I'll never forget it.

Second, I have to thank the women who indulged me, encouraged me, and told me what I could be doing better. Michelle, who somehow believed that I could write a dystopian story, even though I had never done so before, and Beatriz and Rachel, who always say yes when I ask them to read my half-finished projects, and to Penina for reading a later draft. Thank you to Leah, who went back-and-forth with me about a million little details that Google couldn't give the answers to. Thank you to Maya for brainstorming with me what this world might look like and also for fueling my insanity with chocolate chip cookies, apple crisp, and peach pie.

Thank you to Jaded Ibis Press for taking a chance on me, especially to Elizabeth, Vanessa, and Seth. And as always with genre fiction, I stand on the shoulders of giants. Thank you to Suzanne, Christine, George, Margaret, and anyone else who came before me. I see you, and I see your presence in my own work.

Perhaps most importantly, thank you to those creating waves in real life, the people speaking up and out for Black and brown lives, for indigenous rights, for queer and trans folks, for immigrant rights, for women around the world. You make a difference, and the world is a better place because of you.

CPSIA information can be obtained
at www.ICGtesting.com
Printed in the USA
FSHW011933300621
82852FS